INTO HELL...

The familiar odor met him at the doorway—and it almost stopped him from going in. . . . There was no mistaking that smell, once it had been experienced.

Bolan sent 200 pounds of enraged kick into the flimsy door and stepped quickly inside with the same motion. A guy at the far window looked around with a sick grin and immediately elevated both hands in quick surrender . . . but some things simply cannot be surrendered. The big silver pistol thundered from the doorway to send 240 grains of howling death splattering through that sick grin.

Another guy ran in from a back room just in time to catch the next round in the jugular. Most of his throat sprayed away with the hit, but the guy just stood there for a frozen moment while the brain tried to understand the message. Another quick round plowed in between unbelieving eyes to correct the sloppy hit and verify the unhappy message.

And Bolan now had the full attention of the figure in a blood-spattered vinyl smock. "I can explain," he declared. It was not the voice one would expect from a maniac, but calm, cultured—almost detached from the horror at hand.

Bolan replied, "Good for you," and blew away the devil's elbow. The guy screamed and grabbed for a tourniquet that lay on the table beside his victim. The next round from the AutoMag blew his wrist away and another quickly followed to the knee. *There were times when killing wasn't enough. . . .*

THE EXECUTIONER SERIES

the EXECUTIONER #35

WEDNESDAY'S WRATH

by Don Pendleton

PINNACLE BOOKS   LOS ANGELES

EXECUTIONER #35: WEDNESDAY'S WRATH

An original Pinnacle Books edition, published for the first time anywhere.

First printing, May 1979

ISBN: 0-523-40335-6

Cover illustration by Gil Cohen

Printed in the United States of America

PINNACLE BOOKS, INC.
2029 Century Park East
Los Angeles, California 90067

Dedicated, with sincere respect, to the men and women of White Sands, birthplace of America's missile and space activity.

Well done. Keep on.

The wrath of the lion
is the wisdom of God.
—William Blake *(Proverbs of Hell)*

Wednesday's child is full of woe,
Thursday's child has far to go.
—Nursery Rhyme

The wrath of the lion
may see me through Wednesday
But where the hell do I go
after that?
—Mack Bolan, the Executioner

PROLOGUE

He could not remember a time when he had not been tired. And "tired" was far too mild a word to describe the way Mack Bolan felt at the moment. It was not mere weariness of the physical systems; Bolan's very soul was at the point of total exhaustion.

Eternal warfare could do that to a guy, of course. But it was more than that, too.

Futility? Was that the word? Was he simply allowing himself to become overwhelmed by the seeming ability of the shit machines to quickly reassemble themselves, no matter what he hit them with? Maybe. A sense of futility could be a terribly grinding thing to the soul of a man who cares.

Army psychologists had characterized him as a man "who commands himself." Exactly what the hell did that mean? What it meant, maybe, depended upon the quality of command.

The *quality* of *command?*

A good commander would take into consideration the capability of his forces—their natural limit of effectiveness. You wouldn't send a rifle squad against an armored column. Unless you were demented. Or terribly desperate. Or, simply, stupid.

The quality of command, yeah. Command of one's self. Maybe somewhere in there lay the whole secret of what made men tick. Maybe it had something to do with an inner vision of one's own worth. Would a good commander—in command of one's self—assign the self to an impossible, hazardous, and futile task . . . if the inner vision was one of high worth?

Maybe so, yeah—if the situation was desperate enough.

Mack Bolan felt comfortable with himself. That was not the problem. He entertained no suicidal or self-sacrificial tendencies.

The problem, dammit, was that the situation *was* desperate—*terribly* desperate! And Bolan, obviously, was simply not up to the task. He had tried. God knew he had tried. He had hit them everywhere he could find them, with everything he could find to hit them with. And even though he had won every battle, every encounter, he was losing the damned war!

Grinding, yeah. A knowledge like that could grind a man down right into the dust.

Futility.

Don Quixote, fighting the magnificent war of the windmills.

To what damned useful effect?

Brognola had told him: "You've won. Try to understand it—you've won! The rest is mere mop-up. Let *us* take care of that."

Sure. It was all over . . . except for a routine mop-up. Bolan had bought that. He'd bought it. Not because it was true, but because he'd *wanted* to buy it. He was tired and he was weary of war and he was sick of commanding the self through an endless succession of meaningless victories and he was lonely and he was damned and he was full to the throat with other men's blood and numb in the heart with too many sacrificial victims to this all-consuming miserable goddamn senseless war!

And, yeah, he was feeling goddamn sorry for the self, too, wasn't he?

So he'd bought Brognola's offer of total amnesty for the sorry self and an end to the unending war. With a tiny reservation. Sop for the soul, Bolan? What else. A six-day blitz, or so he'd thought, to put a final seal on the insidious shit machines. Then the feds could have what was left.

What was *left?* Really?

Sop, yeah. It had sounded so good, so right. The perfect way out, maybe, for a weary soul? *You can't win this war, guy. So do the next best thing. Let someone convince you that you've won so you can turn your back on the reassembly and walk away with head high and feeling good.*

He'd almost managed to do that.

Brognola called it a second-mile effort—more sop—and the head fed arranged military air transport for Bolan's battle cruiser and even provided a pretty assistant to keep it cool. The first day of that "second mile" had been a perfect sop bowl . . . a few minor leaguers from the Midwest ineptly trying a reassembly . . . and Bolan had walked away from that one feeling right and holy.

Day Two had begun with all the promise of Day One—a few broken-down old mobsters grubbing in the ruins of the western syndicate, an easy tap for an Executioner with sop on the mind . . . until he ran head-on into the most monstrous damned reassembly operation the technological mind could conceive. That had shaken the sop bowl just a bit . . . but only just a bit.

Now it was Wednesday . . . Day Three of the Sop Express. Except that now the bowl was gone. It had shattered in the hands and disappeared like the wisp it had been all along. The schedule had called for a quick visit to Dallas and a freeze-dried look at the remnants of the Texas mob. The warwagon had been airlifted ahead under the care of April Rose, the "pretty assistant" and new custodian of Bolan's Sop. And then, moments before Bolan's own scheduled departure with a fresh supply of armaments, the hot flash had come down from Leo Turrin, Bolan's inside man at La Commissione, the mob's New York headquarters.

4

So here sat Mack Bolan—not in Mile Two Dallas but in the windswept wastes of New Mexico, grimly contemplating the saddle of the devilhorse, which would carry him with a single leap back to the gates of hell, back to war eternal, back to the infinite vista of Mile One: War Unending Against the Mafia.

And he was so tired.

God knew, he was weary to the soul.

CHAPTER ONE

INTO HELL

The familiar odor met him at the doorway—and it almost stopped him from going in. The one thing Mack Bolan did not need at this moment was another living nightmare. And there was no mistaking that smell, once it had been experienced. But then the nightmare groaned, and there was also no way to turn away from that.

He sent 200 pounds of enraged kick into the flimsy door and stepped quickly inside with the same motion. The thing on the table at room center was far beyond any awareness of that entry. And the ghoul who was bending over it was too engrossed in his art to take note of anything else. But a guy at the far window looked around with a sick grin and immediately elevated both hands in quick surrender to the imposing figure at the door. Some things simply cannot be surrendered. The big silver pistol thundered from the doorway to send 240 grains of howling death splattering through that sick grin.

Another guy ran in from a back room just in time to catch the next round in the jugular. Most of his throat sprayed away with the hit, but the guy just stood there on the back porch of hell for a frozen moment while the brain tried to understand the message. Another quick round plowed in between unbelieving eyes to correct the sloppy hit and verify the unhappy message.

And Bolan now had the full attention of the maniac in the blood-spattered vinyl smock. The guy was about fifty, tall and spare of frame, handsome with a touch of distinguishing gray at the temples, and very nicely dressed beneath the protective vinyl. "I can explain," declared the turkeymaster. It was not the voice one would expect from a maniac, but calm, cultured—almost detached from the horror at hand.

Bolan replied, "Good for you," and blew away the devil's elbow.

The guy screamed and grabbed for a tourniquet that lay on the table beside his victim. The next round from the AutoMag blew his wrist away and another quickly followed to the knee.

The turkeymaster hit the floor, squawling and writhing for a comfort that was not going to be found. He lay there jerking around in his own blood, for a change, screaming for a mercy he had never accorded others.

A turkeymaster Mack Bolan was not. He'd never hit for pain or punishment—and the shock of those massive hits would not, he knew, produce anything near the mind-cracking agony and helpless horror that this guy had been systematically dealing out to others. Just the same, the guy was hurting like hell and the sounds of that suffering were getting to Bolan's belly. But maybe the guy needed to take to hell with him some small appreciation of what he'd been handing out so freely to others—and someone else was first in line for Sergeant Mercy.

The thing on the table was only marginally alive and blessedly unconscious. Doc Turkey had apparently been trying to bring that shredded mind back into conscious focus. There was no way to know at a glance whether it had been male or female—or, for that matter, black or white, human or otherwise. It was simply a *thing*—torched, carved, scraped and hacked into a mutilated and shapeless lump—that had been kept alive and, no doubt, aware throughout most of its ordeal.

There was no way to reverse that nightmare or to even salvage anything from it. Bolan muttered, "Go find peace," and put a bullet where an ear had been. Then he turned to the squawling monster on the floor and sent him the same mercy.

Bolan found another gruesome turkey when he checked the back room. This one had been dead for some time—hours, perhaps.

Bolan was shaking the joint down for intelligence when Jack Grimaldi moved inside, a short shotgun cradled at the chest.

"Jesus *Christ!*" the pilot muttered and quickly went back outside.

"Is it cool?" Bolan called to him through the open doorway.

"It's cool, yeah," was the strained reply. "What is that in there?"

Bolan went on with his search as he called back, "It's a turkey shack."

"Aw, shit," Grimaldi groaned. "Really? Aw, no. I thought that was just a myth. Hcy, I didn't know I was bringing those poor bastards to—I really didn't know!"

"It's no myth," Bolan growled. "And you couldn't have changed a thing, Jack. Did you check out the vehicle?"

"Yeah. Clean. Keys in the ignition. It's from Alamogordo."

Bolan went to the doorway and leaned tiredly against the jamb. "Okay. Thanks again, buddy. I'm releasing you. I'll take the car into town."

"It's your game," the pilot quietly replied. "But, you know, you can fly me anywhere. I can think of lots of places better for you right now than Alamogordo. Almost anywhere, in fact."

They'd been good friends since the Caribbean adventure, and more than that. As a mob pilot, Grimaldi had been a steady source of reliable intelligence and he'd risked a lot—he'd risked everything—as a Bolan convert and ally.

The Executioner smiled at his friend the Mafia

pilot as he told him, "Thanks for the thought. Save the worry for yourself." He inclined his head toward the nightmare behind him. "That's what they do to their *friends,* guy."

Grimaldi shivered and turned his gaze elsewhere. "Sunrise soon," he said.

Bolan said, "Soon, yeah. You'd best move it out. Now."

"You're mad as hell, aren't you?"

The tall man in the doorway smiled tightly as he replied, "I can handle it."

"Listen . . . I'll fly on over to Alamogordo and tie down there for the day. I'll leave my hotel address with the base operator. If you should need some quick wings . . ."

Bolan said, "Thanks. I'll keep it in mind."

Grimaldi hesitated for a moment then asked, sotto voce, "Who were the turkeys?"

"You don't really want to know."

"I guess not, no. Okay. Well, I'll be around." The pilot turned away and strode off across the wastelands.

Sunrise soon, yeah. Already the black of night had deteriorated to a dirty gray. Bolan watched his friend disappear into that grayness, then he went back inside the shack and resumed the search. He loaded a tape recorder and several used tapes into the vehicle parked just outside, then threw in a collection of wallets and other personal items gathered during the shakedown.

Ten minutes after Grimaldi had set off on his

10

solo return trek to the plane, the nightmare shack was in flames and Mack Bolan was beginning his journey into another nightmare in the appropriated Mafia wheels.

Grimaldi flew over the burning shack and dipped his wings in a silent farewell. Bolan responded with a flash of headlights and quickly put that scene behind him.

The physical scene, that is.

The images would remain with him to the grave. Worse yet, he'd have to listen to those abominable tapes—the record of two souls descending into hell itself. The turkey techniques made brainwashing a genteel social affair by comparison. It was not brainwashing, but soul bursting. Interspersed with all the shrieks and desperate pleas would be the babblings of a life record in quick and selective playback—containing every sin imagined or otherwise, along with everything else a desperate soul could devise to please its tormentor, so as to shut off that which was already recognized as irreversible.

Yeah, Bolan would have to listen to all that.

And yes, Jack, he was already mad as hell. Not so much because of *who* they were, but simply *because* they were.

Bolan had no particular sense of compassion for the likes of Charlie Rickert and Jack Lamamafria, the latter also known lately as Jack Lambert.

But nobody deserved to die that way. Not even with the fate of the entire civilized world hanging

11

in the balance. Did that sound melodramatic? Too bad, then. Because that was precisely the point of this latest game in the troubled life of Mack Bolan: the fate of the entire civilized world.

CHAPTER TWO

THE SWIRL

Bolan heard enough from the tapes during the hour's drive into Alamogordo to confirm his guess that the movements in New Mexico were directly related to the recent developments he had just left behind in California. Rickert and Lamamafria had been charged with the security of that West Coast operation, which had been ripped asunder by Bolan's Day Two mop-up of the area. There were overtones of punishment for a responsibility poorly met during the interrogations, but the main thrust had obviously been total recall in an outrageously inhuman "debriefing" of the two Mafia lieutenants. Which merely underscored the importance with which the higher bosses regarded the events of yesterday in California—and especially as they were related to the New Mexico thing.

It was not exactly standard form to so punish

an honest failure; in fact, Bolan had never heard of such an occurrence in the past. Such treatment was traditionally reserved for traitors or enemies with important secrets. It was beyond doubt, though, that these tapes constituted a debriefing of friendly personnel carried to unusual extremes.

Something very big was developing, for sure.

Muted rumblings of that something had been emanating from the area for some time. In fact, Bolan had followed the tremors from his recent blast into Arizona and had been tentatively scouting the New Mexico question when the urgent summons from the East sent him airlifting into Tennessee. All he'd found during that brief probe had been whispers and echoes of some quiet underworld activity in the wastelands. Now here he was again, same scene, probably the same situation, except that now the whispers had become shrieks of agony.

But a pattern was developing, for sure.

The flash from Leo Turrin had warned of a "large event" going down in New Mexico—related somehow to the California disaster—with various "important men" hastily dispatched to that area.

As another item in the weave, Charlie Rickert and Lamamafria were the only ranking local members of the California conspiracy to survive Bolan's rampage in Los Angeles. Bolan had last seen Lamamafria, a.k.a. Jack Lambert, lying unconscious on the floor of his Sunset District

14

office. Rickert, the renegade cop, had been turned over to local authorities after assuring Bolan that he would cooperate.

According to Leo Turrin, who had not been in a position to get it all, someone had "moved heaven and earth to spring a certain VIP prisoner from the L.A. county jail"—and this was somehow related to the thing in New Mexico.

Big Tim Braddock, a recent convert to the Bolan cause and now deputy chief of the L.A. cops, was all but frothing at the mouth as he confirmed Bolan's suspicion that Charlie Rickert's release had, indeed, been quietly engineered, mere hours following his arrest.

Then Jack Grimaldi had provided the cinching element with his report of "ferrying a burial party" from Santa Monica to a lonely spot in the New Mexico wastelands.

"Two pigeons," Grimaldi reported to his old friend, "with two keepers. They had 'em doped and hooded all the way so I don't know who the poor bastards are. There was a car waiting for them, in the middle of nowhere. I had to land on a dirt road in the dark, without lights if you can imagine that."

Bolan had imagined that, yeah. And he'd asked his friend, the Mafia pilot, to repeat the performance. Now it seemed that Leo's fears had been right on target. Something big was going down, for sure. It was directly related to the California thing. Maybe it was an action-reaction sequence. That would explain all the urgent parleys in New York while the Los Angeles thing was falling apart.

Yeah, maybe so.

It was now very obvious that the council of bosses—weak though their coalition might be at the moment—had not been all that concerned about outsider Bill McCullough and his ambitious stretch toward a West Coast takeover. The vaunted "California Concept" had probably been at their fingertips the whole while, awaiting nothing more than the proper moment for the cannibals to step in and make it their own. Until Bolan happened onto it. But they'd not been concerned about McCullough. They'd had Rickert and Lamamafria inside that operation right at the top.

And it was guys like McCullough who kept the mob fat, happy, and immortal—even at a moment when you'd think they were going down for the final count.

Mack Bolan should have remembered that.

And he should have remembered the litany of the Mafia:

> If you can't steal it, extort it;
> If you can't extort it, join it;
> If you can't join it, corrupt it;
> If you can't corrupt it, hit it;
> If you can't hit it, buy it;
> After you've got it, eat it.
> And if you can't get it, eat it on the run.

16

Yeah. You could say what you like about the Italian brotherhood—whatever else, they were the most persistent and successful cannibals of them all—and people in Bill McCullough's league should have learned that long ago.

People like Hal Brognola and Mack Bolan should not have forgotten it. The American mob was not down for the count. They'd bounced back with amazing resiliency. If Bolan could not stop them here, quickly and resoundingly, then he might as well forget the briefly ignited hopes for an end to this damnable war. It would go on for as long as Mack Bolan lived. Which, of course, *could* mean for only another hour or two . . . all things considered.

CHAPTER THREE

IMAGES

The turkeyman was using the name Philip Jordan and his spanking new driver's license gave the address of a modern apartment complex in Alamogordo. Bolan drove past the place in a slow pass to a small shopping center a few blocks beyond. The day was still quite young, though, and none of the stores were open, but he found a public telephone at the edge of the parking lot and made three quick long distance calls. He spoke briefly to contacts in Los Angeles, Dallas, and New York, then went on to a small, all-night grocery and made a few purchases.

It was nearing eight o'clock when he returned to the apartment building. The place was now stirring with life—since it was the time of day when most people were beginning their daily work routine. Bolan remained in the car for several minutes, getting the feel of the place. Two men and three women, all young, entered the parking area during that period, got into cars, and went their separate ways. That and other quiet clues combined to present the picture of an abode for singles. The general layout was of three moderate-sized buildings, grouped around a small swimming pool and patio, with tennis courts at the rear and parking for about fifty cars. That parking lot now held no more than a dozen vehicles; apparently most of the tenants were off about their daily business.

Bolan lit a cigarette and studied the layout until he was pretty well oriented, then he gathered his stuff and went directly to Jordan's apartment. It was at patio level, opposite the pool. A quick glance at the lock provided the clue to the proper key from Jordan's own key ring. He unlocked the door and stepped inside, with the air of a man who owned the joint.

Small, studio style. One room encompassed living, dining, and kitchen areas—a single small bedroom and bath. But nice enough. Neat and clean. The refrigerator contained milk, eggs, some vegetables and nothing else. Canned soups and vegetables in the cupboard. Brown bread, packaged rice. No cigarettes, no booze, no meats. The guy was an ascetic.

A small table by the couch held a neat stack of magazines. No *Playboys* or *Hustlers*, though. *Scientific American, Psychology Today, Commentary* and several others of that caliber, all current. And all had been forwarded via the mails to

19

Dr. Philip Jordan from a Maryland address. Uh huh.

Wastebaskets were empty and clean—even in the bathroom. The trash compactor in the kitchen area held a fresh bag with nothing in it.

Bolan was beginning to wonder if anyone actually lived there.

But there was a neat array of toilet articles, partially used tubes and bottles, occupying the bathroom chest. A laundry hamper in the bedroom closet contained two barely soiled towels, two pairs of socks, two sets of underwear, two white shirts. Clean suits, shirts, and an assortment of subdued ties hung neatly in the closet.

Neat and clean, yeah. Bolan was remembering that calm look, the cultured voice, the careful attire. And he was projecting that image into this apartment, developing an insight into the man who had called this place home—a well-educated, handsome man in his forties or early fifties, unmarried or at least living alone at the moment, fussily tidy, practically ascetic and almost antiseptic in lifestyle, perhaps a vegetarian and almost certainly an intellectual. *Doctor* Philip Jordan. Doctor of what? Besides turkeys.

Bolan returned to the stack of magazines and went through them carefully. He scored four hits in the area of human psychology. Okay. Maybe it fit.

Bolan carried his stuff into the bathroom, started a fresh tape in the recorder, and began transforming himself into a reasonable facsimile

20

of Dr. Philip Jordan. He listened intently to the tonal inflections of the only calm voice on that tape while he shaved and prepared the physical image. There was no thought toward a precise duplication—nor would that have been possible. Bolan was going for the *role* image—which, he hoped, should be enough. Jordan did not appear to be the sort of man with close personal ties. He obviously had not been living in the area for very long. And he was certainly not the type of guy you'd find cozying up to the earthy Mafia people. Aloof to the point of haughtiness, stiff, formal— or that was the way Bolan was reading the guy.

And, yes, if it were a true reading then perhaps the role image would be enough to turn the trick.

If not . . . well, everybody dies somewhere.

He rubbed in a bit of cosmetic shadow to emphasize the cheekbones and darken the eyes a bit, formed a collodion wrinkle between the brows, restyled the hair and combed in some white at the temples. Then he watched the image in the mirror and found the facial feel of a haughty intellectual, who felt just a bit above everyone around him.

He turned off the tape recorder, having heard too damned much already. But he had the voice. It would be a cinch.

He was getting into a suit of the guy's clothes and finding the fit when the first telephone call came. It was the Dallas connection.

"Okay, I've got your man," the worried tones of Hal Brognola told him. "I've checked out your line there. It's clean. But I'm not so sure I want to give you this stuff. We'd all a lot rather you just leave New Mexico to us. I can get you a jet airlift out of there within thirty minutes. That would put you in Dallas in plenty of time to—"

"Save it, Hal," Bolan tiredly broke in. "Dallas will keep. This will not. What do you have?"

He could hear the guy breathing unhappy fumes for a moment before that agitated voice sighed in capitulation. "The name's for real. He's been living in a suburb of Washington until recently."

Bolan lit a cigarette and asked his friend, the fed, "What's he a doctor of?"

"Foul play."

"What?"

"He's got a Ph.D. from Georgetown but he's no philosopher, friend. The defense department canned him two years ago. He was a psych war specialist."

It fit, yeah. "Why'd they fire him?" Bolan wondered aloud.

"Rank insubordination, says here. Which probably means he was out of control. Sensitive employee status . . . think tanks."

Bolan said, "Uh huh. Okay. What aren't you telling me?"

Brognola sighed heavily into the connection. Presently he replied, "For some reason the CIA picked right up on the guy. He was on their payroll until a few weeks ago."

"Doing what?"

"I'm still awaiting that answer," Brognola replied.

"Why'd they let him go?"

"I'm awaiting that, too."

"That tight, eh?"

"Yeah."

Bolan said, "The guy's a turkey doctor, Hal."

A long silence occupied the line, then: "You're sure of that?"

"Caught 'im with red hands," Bolan replied drily. "I suppose you can guess who the prime turkey was."

Brognola growled, "Rickert, huh?"

"That's the one."

"I don't get that. Why?"

"That's what I'm trying to find out, Hal."

"Dammit." Another silent pause, then: "Well there goes our Los Angeles key."

"Maybe not," Bolan said. "I'm, uh, working the problem, Hal. I'll want some distant support."

"Name it."

"A computer search, I guess. Anything anomalous in the southwestern region. Installations, personnel, all of it."

"What, uh, the hell are you. . . ? Even computers have—"

"Sorry," Bolan said quickly. "My mind is working faster than my mouth. I think of New Mexico and I wonder where the hell is the picnic—and all I get back is top secret stamps. White Sands. Los Alamos. Could it relate to our Los Angeles problem. You know the routine?"

Brognola growled, "I guess I do, yeah. We'll give the computers a shake and see what falls out."

"Okay. I'll try to get back to you in a couple of hours. Would that give you time enough?"

"I guess it all depends," Brognola replied. "We'll give it a fit, though. And you watch your ass, buddy. Keep it forever in sight. I don't want to lose you this close to the gate."

Bolan chuckled solemnly as he told his old friend, "I'll try to keep that in mind."

"You want me to dispatch your battleship? The lady is pacing holes in the floor. I don't know if I can . . ."

"I don't want her here just yet," Bolan replied quietly. The lady referred to was, of course, the one and only April Rose. She had the warwagon in custody . . . along with Mack Bolan's heart. And he could understand her anxiety. But, no, he certainly did not wish to have her mixing into this thing—not at this stage, especially. "Send the cruiser to El Paso for now. That puts it within quick call."

"Okay. I'll have it at Fort Bliss before noon. Hit her floater as soon as you can, though. You know what I mean."

Bolan knew what Brognola meant, yeah. April was not exactly predisposed to sitting and waiting for things to happen. Especially if she was worried about her man. Bolan sighed and told the fed, "Keep her busy, Hal. Let her understand the

24

importance of this computer run. And turn her loose on it. She's damn good at that."

"Among other things," Brognola added drily. "Okay. Are we clear for now?"

"Almost. What about this turkey doctor? Does he have any medical background?"

Brognola said no, then changed his mind. "Wait—yeah, a little. Nearly two years of medical school before he switched to psychology. I guess you could call that a background."

Yes, Bolan guessed that you could. He said, "Later," and hung up.

And just in time.

The phone rang again almost immediately and a harsh voice at the other side growled, "We been waitin' for you to call."

Bolan pitched his response cool and aloof. "Your wait would have been rewarded had you awaited another minute."

"We been waitin' all night, Doc. Did you get it or didn't you?"

"I have it," replied Bolan, the turkey doctor.

"So what're you waiting for? Bring it over. We'll expect you in ten minutes."

"Absolutely not," Bolan said coolly. "I'll meet you halfway. Name the place."

The man at the other end chuckled as he replied, "You CIA guys kill me. Okay. Would Stan's Drive-In suit you? Say five minutes?"

"Say fifteen," Bolan replied coldly and hung up. But he was feeling a bit troubled as he strapped on the Beretta shoulder rig, and finished dressing. Had he blundered into a CIA covert operation? Surely not. But he remembered a couple of CIA types he'd known at Saigon, and . . .

But . . . a turkey doctor?

Brognola did not yet have a complete file on the guy. Which meant he'd have to penetrate a few security interlocks to complete the file, no simple task for even an official in Brognola's position.

Leo Turrin had never heard of the guy, either. Which meant not a hell of a lot in a positive sense, but at least was negatively encouraging.

It was going to be a crap shoot, for sure.

Bolan was betting everything he had on nothing more than a gut feeling that Philip Jordan was not well-known by his Mafia playmates. A guy with Jordan's background would be cagey and careful. Personal meetings with known criminals would therefore be conducted furtively, quickly—in places like dark bars or parked cars, where lighting was bad and vision minimal.

Yeah, he was betting his life on that. And on the naturally poor perceptual capabilities of most people.

The dead man's clothing was not a perfect fit, either, but it would have to be close enough. Bolan gave both the image and the voice a final checkout, then picked up the tapes and went out of there.

Hell, it was the only move he had.

CHAPTER FOUR

CONNECTIONS

The meeting point was just a few blocks from the Jordan apartment. Bolan had noticed the place earlier while looking for a public phone. It was a small drive-in restaurant occupying a remote corner on one of the city's thoroughfares, a rather nondescript sandwich place, which did not cater to breakfast appetites. It would not open until time for the lunch trade.

Bolan's appropriated vehicle was the only one on the lot. He pulled across several parking lanes and halted with the car poised for a quick out. A dusty station wagon immediately swung out of a service station on the opposite corner and bounced into the drive-in.

Bolan slipped on dark glasses and rolled down his window as the wagon pulled alongside his vehicle.

Three guys were in there, all casually dressed,

all definitely Mafia. Two of them moved quickly into Bolan's vehicle, one sliding in beside him and the other to the rear.

Without a word he sent the car onto the street and rolling slowly toward downtown. The dusty station wagon pulled out and fell in behind. And the guy at Bolan's elbow was sharing some quiet, secret joke with the one in the rear seat.

Bolan intoned, "Smile all you wish, gentlemen. Discretion is still the saving grace of our business."

These guys were fairly young, mean-looking, energetic. But they were having a good time with the CIA guy.

The one beside Bolan said, "Sure, Doc. We're just smiling because we're happy. Right, Nick?"

The guy in the back seat said, "Right. But what about the two boys from L.A., Doc?"

Bolan smiled solemnly into the rear view mirror as he replied, "Okay. What about them?"

"Well, where are they?"

"Are you referring to the keepers or to the kept?"

The guy in front laughed at that and picked up the package of tapes. He rattled it and said, "We know all about the *kept*. Right, Nick?"

Bolan said, "I hope you held no special affection for the keepers."

The guy shot a quick look to the rear and replied, "What does that mean?"

Bolan gave him a direct gaze for the first time. It was just a quick flick of the eyes from behind smoked glasses, but it was enough to convey the hidden meaning. "It means I hope you held no special affection," he said.

The guy in the back snickered.

The one beside Bolan coughed delicately into his hand and said, "I didn't even know those boys, Doc."

Bolan said, "Good. You won't miss them, then, will you?" He pulled to the curb. The station wagon pulled on past and parked just ahead. The *Mafioso* at Bolan's elbow was looking troubled and confused. Bolan turned another direct gaze his way and said, "Tell the man I made an executive decision. There was no alternative to a termination with extreme prejudice. He will understand when he plays the tapes."

The guy behind snickered again and said, "I love the fancy names these guys give to a cold hit —don't you, Bean?"

The other one growled, "Shut up, Nick." He pushed his door open, then turned back for a parting word. "Keep yourself available, Doc." That was a command, with no confusion evident. "The captain will want to talk to you about those terminations."

The *captain?*

Bolan said, "He'll know where to find me. But the tapes speak clearly for themselves."

The two men left without further comment and went to their own vehicle.

Bolan gave them a two-block lead, then followed in a loose track. Traffic was extremely light and it was not at all difficult to keep their vehicle in sight. There was no reason for those guys up there to suspect a tail. But they had one. And Mack Bolan was prepared to follow them clear to hell. Or to "the captain"—whichever came first.

A delapidated house in a rundown district on the north side came first—but it was just a quick stop. Only one of the guys went inside and he was back again in a matter of seconds. They then swung over to Route 54 and continued north toward Tularosa.

This was ruggedly beautiful country—a jumble of mountain ranges and soaring peaks, desert areas, lava flows, and all that could mark a land with the cataclysmic violence of geological evolution. Ironic, too, that this landscape so scarred by primal natural violence was mother earth to the greatest unnatural violence ever unleashed. The first A-bomb had been exploded in this region. And that was not the end of irony. To Bolan's left lay the White Sands Missile Range, where are tested the most sophisticated weapons of the technological age; to his right an Apache Indian Reservation, where original Americans continued ancient tribal traditions barely touched by technology.

Bolan had done his homework on New Mexico during that earlier brief visit to the area. And it had become quickly obvious that this was no natural habitat for the species *Mafioso carnivoris*. It simply was not their sort of place. The population density was something like eight people per

30

square mile, as compared with New York's 380. Government workers constituted the largest employee group in the state, with something more than a fourth of the total labor force. There was some agriculture, some mining, some oil and some gas—nothing spectacular there. The spectacular part was the natural scenic beauty, but the tourist trade was not all that great, either.

So what the hell did the boys want here? Where was the pie, the picnic spread? Finally, what was going down in New Mexico now that could be linked to Bill McCullough's pie-in-the-sky movement in California?

An answer was forming, but it was an answer that Mack Bolan did not wish to accept.

He was getting closer to that acceptance, though, with every snick of his tires against the lonely road in this Land of Enchantment . . . and of exotic weapons of war.

It was just a few miles north of Alamogordo where the track abruptly turned west and headed off into the boonie hills toward the White Sands forbidden zone. The path was a dirt road very quietly marked with a small handmade sign, which read: *Rancho Jacundo.*

Bolan slowed and went on past the exit, while keeping his eyes on the dust cloud created by the speeding station wagon. He pulled to the side and halted about a quarter-mile beyond. The target vehicle was no longer visible, but the cloud of dust was. He watched it until it disappeared be-

31

hind the hills—marking that spot with an *X* in his mind—then he turned around and went back to town.

Rancho Jacundo, eh?

Okay. So okay. The rest would take care of the rest.

An older man who was sunning himself on the patio at Jordan's apartment building smiled diffidently and nodded to him as he strolled past.

Bolan smiled back and the guy said, "Beautiful day, Mr. Jordan."

So much for a clean sweep in role images and human perceptions.

"Depends on where you're standing," said Bolan-Jordan and went on before the guy could extend the conversation.

The phone rang as he stepped inside. He scooped it up and announced, "Philip Jordan here."

"We're sending a car for you," declared a new voice. "Cap'n wants your help in analyzing this data."

"Never mind the car," Bolan clipped back. "I'll deliver myself, thanks."

"Not there," said the voice. Meaning, probably, the house in town. "You don't know this place. We'll send—"

"You're at Rancho Jacundo, aren't you?" Bolan said, with a malicious twinkle in the voice.

That gave the guy a moment of pause. Finally he replied, "Pretty goddam cute, aren't you, guy?"

Bolan brushed that aside with the cool response: "I have a couple of matters in town, first. You'll see me within the hour." He hung it up and turned quickly to the realization of another presence in that small apartment, the Beretta leaping forth and leading the way into the pivot.

But there was no valid target there.

And Doc Jordan was not quite the ascetic Bolan had imagined.

A very pretty young lady stood just inside the doorway to the bedroom. She had long black hair reaching almost to the waist, a pleasingly voluptuous torso, and legs enough to delight even an ascetic. She wore only a delicate negligee of lavender lace, open all the way down.

Luminous eyes were grappling with the gun in Bolan's hand as she exclaimed, "Phil! What. . . ?"

But then those magnificent eyes swept upward and traveled the face twice around.

"You're not Phil," she declared in a shaking voice.

No, indeed, he was not.

But the day had become a bit more beautiful, just the same. Or a bit uglier . . . depending on where a guy was standing.

CHAPTER FIVE

PROJECTIONS

Her age was somewhere in that indeterminate
zone between late-twenties and early-thirties, the
eyes bright and expressive, skin like soft copper
and about the same color—a very lovely woman.

Intelligent, too.

She smoothly backpedaled in quiet retreat,
drawing the negligee firmly closed and holding it
there with both hands.

Bolan told her, "We can do this the hard way
or the easy way."

That pert face was composed, but the voice was
scared as hell as she replied, "Let's try easy."

He said, "Sit down."

She stiffly lowered herself to the edge of the
bed and perched there, as though ready for a
quick flight. Bolan swung a chair around and
straddled it, peering at her over clasped hands

atop the backrest. "Who are you?" he asked in a mild tone.

"My name is Mary Valdez."

"What are you to Philip Jordan?"

"Friend—we're just friends. Good friends."

"Very good friends," Bolan said.

She looked down at the negligee. "That's right."

"How long have you known him?"

"Are you some kind of cop? Because if you are—"

"I thought we were taking it the easy way," he said. "That means that I ask the questions. You supply the answers. Easy way. Okay?"

She shivered and replied, "Okay, sure."

"How long have you known him?"

"About . . . five years, I guess."

"That's a long time."

"Yes."

"Where do you live?"

"I live here. In Alamogordo."

"Since forever?"

"Since forever, yes," she said.

"But Phil's been here for only a few weeks," Bolan pointed out. "How could you have known him for five years?"

"Well, he works for the Pentagon. I work at the test center. That's where we met. At the center, I mean. He's around there a lot."

"A few days at a time, though," Bolan suggested.

"Yes. Well, now, he's been transferred out here."

"To do what?"

"What?"

"Is he working at the center?"

"No. He's . . ." Her eyes flared and worked at the door for a moment. "I don't think I have to answer these questions. Where is Phil? Why are you made up to look like him? What's going on here?"

Bolan said, "That's what I'm trying to find out. I think he's in big trouble. I'm here to find out what it is."

She said, "Oh God," in a miserable little voice and lost the stiff composure. After a moment of silence, she asked him, "Could you show me some credentials or something?"

He shook his head and firmly replied, "No way."

The lady cried a little, then, and fussed with the negligee a lot.

Bolan went to the bathroom, wet the end of a towel, and gave it to her. She accepted with a grateful sweep of wet eyes and went to work on the face.

When she'd got it back together, she said, "You're from Washington, aren't you?"

He lied a little. "Yes. But if you want to help me, then let's pretend I'm totally dumb. I know nothing. Tell me what I ought to know."

"What can I tell you?"

"Where has Phil been working these past few weeks?"

"I don't know if I can tell you that."

"There's no choice, lady. You have to tell me that."

She dabbed at her face some more, then said, "Well, I sort of believe he's on some special assignment."

"You mean like, maybe, for the CIA."

Those expressive eyes jumped at that. She said, "Maybe. He did some field work for the CIA a few years ago. But that was overseas. The CIA doesn't work—I was thinking maybe G-Two or something."

"He's done field intelligence for the army before?"

"Oh yeah. Sure. Lots of that."

Bolan told her, "That's fine, Mary. That's very good. We have a start. Now let's keep it on this level. Has he been spending any time out at the test center lately?"

"Not much. He was at Fort Bliss for a couple of days. That was . . . two weeks ago. Then he went . . . I think he went to Los Alamos once. And he was at Holloman. He's been very busy. I've actually seen very little of him this time."

"But you were expecting him to be here today."

"Yes. We—he said—we had a date." She plucked at the negligee and pitched her voice to a near whisper. "He said I should come on in and make myself comfortable. He'd be here about ten - -about ten o'clock."

Bolan observed, "You're pretty early, then."

"Yes, well, I thought—I wanted to make myself pretty and—and surprise him."

Bolan said, "Congratulations. You look very pretty. And you surprised the *hell* out of *me.*"

The lady actually smiled a little as she told him, "You *scared* it out of *me!*"

He grinned and offered her a cigarette. She declined. He started to light one for himself, then changed his mind and quietly asked her, "You know nothing about Phil's assignment? I mean, the *real* assignment, not the cover."

She sucked in her breath and shook the pretty head. "Just what I told you. I knew something was off key, though. But he didn't—we aren't— Phil and I are not all that tight. You know what I mean."

"Just friends," Bolan said, smiling.

She smiled back. "Right. That's right."

"When was he at the center last?"

"That would be . . . Monday, I guess. This is Wednesday? Monday, right."

"His executive clearance is still in force, then," Bolan said casually.

"Well, sure. Why wouldn't it be?"

He stood up and twirled his chair about, dropped back onto it, and leaned toward the bed with elbows on his knees. The voice was pitched low and confidential when he said, "This is—I shouldn't tell you this. Can I tell you this?"

The lady solemnly nodded her head and bent forward until their heads were almost touching. "I'm cleared all the way," she assured him.

He took one of her hands and massaged it gently as he told her, "Department of Defense fired

38

Phil two years ago. He isn't even cleared for the janitor's mop bucket."

"That is not possible," she whispered furiously. "I should know. My job is administrative security."

He said, "Right, that's just the point. You *should* know."

She hissed, "What the hell is going on here?"

Bolan said, "You've been had."

"You're crazy! What are you saying?"

"I'm saying the guy has been with the CIA for the past two years. Right now he's with nobody. He's a free agent."

The lady was scared as hell. And too stunned to function. She whispered, "But how . . . how. . . ?"

"You say his clearance is intact. You're sure of that."

"Yes, I'm sure," she replied woodenly. "He's still executive DOD in my book. You say—two *years?* My God. No, it couldn't be. You're wrong. If you're not, then it's some kind of cover operation. I'll bet it's G-Two. He's a security fink. My God, he's set me up! I don't believe—I can't . . ."

"Forget all that crap!" Bolan snarled, trying to snap her out of the fuzzies. "The guy isn't *checking* security, dammit, he's *waltzing* it. What has he been doing out there at the missile test center?"

"He's been auditing my records," she replied, the voice all hollow and dead.

"Meaning exactly what?"

"I'm the security administrator," she said list-

39

lessly. "My branch handles all the clearance data. We coordinate the inter-agency security checks, issue personnel badges, all that. All that."

Bolan said, "Which means he has had complete access to the security clearance system."

She replied, in a faint whisper, "That's what it means."

Bolan stood up and said, "Well, that's just dandy."

The lady began to cry again. Bolan let her. After about forty seconds of that, she started getting mad. "Well, I'm in a hell of a mess, aren't I!" she yelled.

"Is that all that's bothering you?" he said disgustedly.

"Is that *all* that. . . !" She leapt to her feet and let go with a haymaker from far right field. Bolan caught the wrist and held on. She tried to knee him and that was too much. He tossed her back onto the bed and went to a neutral corner, arms folded across the chest, glaring at her with genuine anger.

"You guys are setting me up!" she cried.

He said, "Nuts. You set yourself up. You allowed friendship to override the security routine. You let a guy with two years off the job keep on—"

"What's going on here?" she screamed. "I think I'm going crazy! What the hell kind of—I'm not buying any of this *shit!* You guys aren't going to . . ." She bounced off the bed, ripped the negligee from that luscious body, and flung it at Bolan.

40

"I scream rape in just five seconds if you're still here! We'll see who gets the final shaft in this lousy, damn—"

Bolan gritted his teeth and let her have it once, with an open palm, not hard but just hard enough to lay her back onto the bed. Then he covered her with the torn negligee and told her, "We were going to do this the easy way, Mary."

She rolled onto her belly and began bawling again. Bolan felt like a bastard, and he was. But a bastard he had to be. It was that kind of game.

He pulled the weeping beauty from the bed and into his arms, cuddling and comforting that soft nudity and making reassuring noises in her ear.

After a little of that she began responding to the attention, her sobs becoming soft sighs and quiet little protests.

"I'm your friend," he told her.

"I believe you," she whispered. "I *want* to believe you."

"I have to go out. Will you stay for a couple of hours? Will you cover for me?"

"Cover what?" she sighed.

"For a little while," he explained, "my name is Philip Jordan. I may need some verification of that. For just a little while."

"I guess I could do that," the aroused woman whispered. "Then what?"

"Then I'll scratch your back," he told her.

"That's what friends are for," she said.

"That's what I always say."

"What about Phil?"

"Phil is dead," he said quietly.

The woman stiffened in his arms, pushed herself clear, and sank back onto the bed. "Well, I am very confused," she wearily admitted.

"Welcome to the game," Bolan said. "I'm trying to clear the confusion. But I have to be straight with you, Mary. More is going down here than a security glitch . . . and there's a hell of a lot more to be lost than pride and jobs. You could end up dead. But I do need your help."

She stared at the ceiling and said, "Okay. You've got it. Now get the hell out of here, will you? I need some time. I need more than that. I must look like hell."

"You don't look like hell to me, kid," Bolan truthfully told her. He paused at the door to say, "If you haven't heard from me in a couple of hours, forget it. Everything is off. Get out to the center and pull your own audit on those files. Clean up the act. And blow every damn whistle you can find. Okay?"

She raised herself on an elbow and showed him a wan smile. "Who the hell are you?" she asked solemnly.

"A friend," he said.

"Yeah, yeah," she replied.

Bolan winked at her and went out of there. He had a date with an unknown entity at Rancho Jacundo. And at least now he had a bit more feel for what he was moving into.

And it was, yeah, getting to be an almost beautiful day.

CHAPTER SIX

INTERPRETATIONS

It really was a ranch—or had been, once. But the corrals and cattle chutes were victims of dry rot and had long ago ceased to have any function. Off in the distance, a huddle of adobelike huts could be seen with human figures moving slowly about in some unimaginable mid-morning activity.

The whole place looked like a shot from some Hollywood western—as a hideout for Apache renegades or for a robber band from south of the border. It would be eminently defensible, with natural ramparts of rock formations encircling a small valley in the hills, a zigzag access route through stone canyons.

A movie set, yeah. Bolan would not have been too surprised to find John Wayne standing at the gate.

But this was the late twentieth century—and

what he found was a military jeep bristling with antennae, manned by a GI with MP decals adorning his helmet liner.

Bolan would have been more comfortable with John Wayne. He told the guard, "I'm Dr. Philip Jordan. The captain is expecting me."

The guy responded to that with eyes only and reported the arrival via radio. He then told Bolan, "Park your car at the turnout, sir. Your escort will be here in a minute."

The "escort" was there in less than a minute— another "GI" and another jeep. Nobody requested identification or credentials, though both men wore the standard ID badge and the place was duly posted for "Authorized Access Only."

The ride into the interior was conducted in silence. They skirted south of the adobe huts and ascended a washboard road, which dropped abruptly into a second small valley. This one seemed considerably higher in elevation than the first and technically was not a valley at all but a scooped-out hollow in the shape of a spoon. And that was not the only difference. Here, the motif was strictly military. Large equipment vans and trailers bearing huge dish-antennas were scattered about. These and other installations were concealed from aerial view by a system of camouflage nets. Off to the rear, nestled along the rock walls, were parked a half-dozen or so house trailers of the expandable type, painted in standard camouflage designs. At the center of all that was a large pad for helicopter operations. Two Hueys and several smaller craft now occupied the pad and there was room for considerably more.

Bolan, the warrior, was entertaining a strange sensation at the base of his spine. It was all so damned authentic. Any soldier would feel right at home here. So who was saying that it was *not* authentic? The feeling lingered that he had blundered into some offbeat official operation. Were it not for the constant presence of the mob . . .

He clamped off the spinal shivers and stepped to the ground. The driver had halted the jeep at one of the expanded trailers. The guy had hardly looked at him, but now he smiled almost shyly and tossed his passenger a limp salute as he drove away.

A guy in desert khakis and wearing lieutenant's bars stepped outside to greet him. "Doctor Jordan?" They were a friendly crew. This one, too, grinned as he asked, "How does it look?"

Bolan went up and shook the guy's hand. "Looks great," he said cordially. "Who are you?"

"I'm Thompson, sir."

Bolan said, "Of course," and went inside.

Two young men in military fatigues sat at desks. Neither showed any interest in the visitor. They were fussing with some sort of mathematical data and feeding entries into small computer terminals. The trailer was otherwise stuffed with electronic gear, except for a small office partition at one end.

Thompson was ushering Bolan toward the office while telling him, "The captain's regrets—he

45

had to step out for a minute. He asked me to work the problem with you. He'll try to get back before we're finished."

Bolan moved into the small office and asked, "What is the problem?"

The real problem, he knew, was entirely his own. He was deep in enemy territory, surrounded by a couple of miles of hostile forces, pretending to be someone he was not—and with almost total ignorance as to who the enemy really was.

Thompson was saying, "It's just a couple of hot spots in the interrogation of Mr. Rickert. Or, actually, a possibility of error in the interpretations. The captain merely wants you to verify the interpretations. Make yourself comfortable, please. I've prepared a transcript of the questionable areas."

Bolan took a seat and Thompson handed him a clipboard with some typewritten sheets attached. The guy was so damned militarily correct, so proper, so . . .

He was saying, "You'll see that these are particularly critical to the Mack Bolan question. The captain desires no possibility of misinterpretation in those areas. Especially in view of the accelerated timetable."

Very drily, Bolan replied, "Of course."

The guy excused himself and stepped out of the office. The transcript sheets were divided into two columns by a heavy black line down the center. To one side appeared the "testimony" of the "subject." The other side was headed *Interpreta-*

tion, and provided concise summaries of the emotional babblings of a ruptured soul in torment.

Bolan confined his attention to the summaries, having already acquired all the familiarity he desired with the other side. The transcript dealt entirely with Bolan's involvement in the Los Angeles fall. From Rickert's point of view, of course. And it was fairly accurate. Jordan had taken the poor bastard through it over and over again, going on to other matters and then returning abruptly to rephrase the same questions time and again. The guy may have been a medical student with a Ph.D. in psychological systems, but he was also a skilled interrogator with all the finesse of a good trial lawyer.

And, yeah, these people were damned concerned about the interests and activities of one Mack Bolan.

The one and only Mack Bolan got to his feet and dropped the transcripts to the desk. He was in a perilous and indefensible position. It had been a critical error to come out here cold, this way. This entire place smelled of Philip Jordan and his style of intrigue. It was not a typical Mafia operation and therefore not subject to the rationale that allowed Bolan to masquerade as Jordan. This "captain," whoever he was, could be a bosom buddy of the dead man. Any of these people out here could be intimately familiar with the renegade DOD executive.

Thompson was speaking in low tones to the other two men when Bolan stepped into the equipment room. He looked up with a smile and said, "That was quick."

"Your interpretations are brilliant," Bolan told him. "Run it that way."

The guy smiled and said, "Great. Would you like some coffee? The captain should—"

Bolan brushed the offer away with an imperious wave of the hand. "My regrets to the captain, there just isn't time for sitting around. I have a thousand things to do."

The smile gave way to a troubled frown. "Well, yes sir, but I believe he wanted to skull over this Bolan problem with you."

"Tell him I'm working that problem," Bolan said, firmly moving out of there.

Thompson stepped quickly to get the door for him.

But another guy was coming in.

This one wore flashy civvies. His age was forty-two and his pedigree was third-generation Mafia by way of the Manhattan junglelands. Bolan had him made in a flash, the mental mug file clicking to an instantaneous readout on one Marco Minotti, kid brother and heir to the late Marinello Family lieutenant, Frank Minotti, whom Bolan had executed in his "command strike" against New York.

This guy had never placed eyes on Mack Bolan, but that was not the present worry. The present worry involved the masquerade as Philip Jordan.

Bolan was ready to play quickly to Minotti's

reaction, but Thompson moved in to take the play for himself. He told Minotti, "Well, this is good timing. Have you gentlemen met?" His gaze shifted quickly to Bolan and he went right on with the introduction, as though the question had been purely rhetorical. And Bolan took note of the protocol: deference was to Doctor Jordan. "Architect, this is Banker."

They had code names yet—great. There was special significance in the manner of introduction, as though Thompson was now revealing a long-kept secret. So if Jordan was the architect and Minotti was the banker, then presumably "the captain" and his synthetic military command would be "Builder," or some such.

And Bolan was getting a hell of a sinking feeling as to the identity of this so-far nameless captain.

Minotti was shaking his hand and growling something derogatory about "this CIA jazz."

Thompson smiled indulgently and said to Bolan, "Banker arrived last night. You were, uh, busy at the moment, so—"

The young lord of Manhattan had a very direct way about him, and his manner clearly stated that he did not like word games. He extended a paw toward Bolan and brusquely cut off Thompson's chatty update. "Name's Minotti," he growled.

Bolan accepted the hand and murmured, "Phillip Jordan."

"Yeah, I know, I know. What'd you get out of them tapes?"

"It's cool," Bolan replied quietly. "No cause for panic."

"Panic, hell," the *Mafioso* snorted. "Speak for yourself, Doc. I hope the bastard *is* around. I got a score to settle with that guy."

"Let's settle it elsewhere," Bolan suggested frostily. "First things first."

"Go to hell," said Minotti. "You guys can't walk and chew gum at the same time. And I'll let you in on a little secret, CIA. If that guy *is* around, you damn sure better put him on top of your list of things to do."

Bolan-Jordan stiffly replied, "I'll keep that in mind."

The warlord turned to Thompson to growl, "So where's Harrelson?"

The sinking feeling reached bottom. The captain or the builder, or whatever, had stood up *absentia* to be identified: Franklin P. Harrelson, ex-Captain, U.S. Infantry, now soldier of fortune and master of intrigue, last encountered by Bolan in the Colorado Kill-zone.

And it was, yes, definitely time to be moving along. Before Thompson could reply to Minotti's query, Bolan said, "Good to meet you, Banker. We'll get together later today and firm everything up." His eye caught Thompson's. "Do I walk or ride?"

"I'll get you some wheels," Thompson replied quickly. The look in the eye said that he understood and sympathized with this cultured man's desire to quit the present company without delay.

Bolan said thank you, and stepped outside.

He hardly had time to light a cigarette before the jeep and same driver reappeared and took him aboard.

It was a tense ride out of that joint, and Bolan was sending up a special word of thanks when he got into his own vehicle and put it all behind him.

It would not remain behind, of course.

In the deeper understanding, that joint—or what it represented—lay smack across Mack Bolan's lifelines. There was nothing to the rear, now. All of it lay just ahead—and each beat of the heart was bringing it that much closer.

It was not a beautiful day.

It was Wednesday—and it was quite possibly the last day of the rest of his life.

CHAPTER SEVEN

THE SPREAD

Perhaps the greatest peril ever faced by Mack Bolan during his crimefighting career, and certainly the most daring and imaginative caper, had come by way of Frank Harrelson. The guy had an audacious and savvy mind. He could have been among the finest combat commanders to emerge from the Vietnam experience; instead, he came home under a cloud, in semidisgrace, doomed to a dubious military future.

They'd been friends in 'Nam—of a sort. Harrelson was a commissioned officer, of course, and Bolan was not—so there had always been that artificial barrier standing between them. Even without that, however, they would never have been true friends. Bolan respected the man's military expertise and combat instincts; he did not particularly approve of Harrelson's personal ethics. There was no particular need to do so. Their personal contacts had been few and fleeting. They were not even in the same command. But there had been a time when "Harrelson's Houdinis"—the tag conferred upon his specialty combat teams by an admiring soldiery—had formed the major cutting edge of the army's pacification program in Vietnam. They were a "hit and git" outfit and their successes were the stuff on which legends are built. The outfit was officially known as Pre-Pac Charlie. It had been Pre-Pac Charlie's task to drive wedges into enemy-held territories in advance of the pacification specialists. Sgt. Bolan's tiny PenTeam Able was another of those legend-building units. Able Team's missions were sometimes at the spearhead of the Pre-Pacs; they functioned as scouts, saboteurs, executioners—always operating deeply in enemy country and usually in total isolation from friendly forces.

There were those times, then, when the Pen-Team combined for joint operations with the Pre-Pacs—and it had been inevitable that Bolan and Harrelson were thrown together from time to time.

So, yes, they knew each other. And respected each other. And they had fought each other in Colorado, in a war of a far different sort.

Bolan had stopped Harrelson in Colorado.

He was not that sure that he could do so here, in New Mexico. The Colorado thing had been pure "caper"—bankrolled and sponsored by the mob, sure, but a caper nonetheless.

New Mexico was looking like something quite

different. The old partnership was evidently still there, sure—the Mafia-military combination. But something quite new had been added to form a trinity of intrigue and very possibly a nightmarish result. The new element was, of course, one Philip Jordan. Even though the guy was now dead and out of it, perhaps that had come too late to effect the outcome.

And this guy Harrelson was bad news enough by himself. It was doubtful that he would recognize Mack Bolan in any casual encounter. Bolan was not wearing the same face he'd worn through Vietnam; there had been no personal confrontation in Colorado. All that was beside the point. The guy was a soldier, and a hell of an effective one; whatever else he might be lacking, it would not be guts, genius, or military capability.

He had shown Bolan in Colorado that he could weld the same disciplined, crack combat outfit from civilians as from genuine army personnel. Of course his civilian troopers had doubtless been recruited from veterans of the Vietnam experience. They were not underworld street punks, but battle-tested, disciplined, able warriors—guys who'd found the realities of peace a bit harder to live with than the realities of war—some of them, maybe, simply male romantics to whom the appeal of living dangerously overrode the prospect of humdrum lives.

Some of these people, maybe—like Harrelson —had been Bolan's comrades in that other war, soldiers of the same side. But that fact could have no meaning here, now. They had chosen their "way to go" and Bolan had chosen his.

Thompson . . . now, there was a guy whom Bolan could have known and maybe liked in Vietnam. He was about Bolan's age—educated, intelligent, competent, likeable but with a hard cutting edge, bet on it, where that edge was needed. Bolan was reading Thompson as Harrelson's chief of staff. And, yes, Bolan had served with many like this one.

There would be no joy in fighting such men.

As for all the damned equipment and official trappings—well, Bolan had seen in Colorado, also, the audacious masquerade that had even the Pentagon confused and sucked in. He was probably seeing it again here, in this highly sensitive area of the nation's military resources—but this time, no doubt, greatly enhanced by the special touch of the late Philip Jordan.

A trinity: the architect, Jordan; the procurer, Harrelson's Houdinis; the buyer, Mafiadom as personified in Marco Minotti.

It could be a hellish combination, yeah, whatever the game.

Whatever else this operation might be, it certainly was nothing like the quasimilitary attempt in Arizona via the renegades Hinshaw, Worthy and Morales. Those guys had been no more than street punks, whatever their other experiences, and their thinking had never risen above that level. Harrelson was a different item entirely. So was Jordan. Whatever was going on down here in

New Mexico, it would most certainly be something extravagant, audacious, and maybe even world-shaking.

It was tied in somehow to the California thing.

It was happening in an area where secret military technology was the chief commodity.

So what the hell was the product?

What was the mob *buying* in New Mexico?

So what the hell else, Bolan?

Here was the "pie"—the "picnic spread." Right here, all of it. Here was White Sands, Los Alamos, Holloman Air Force Base, Fort Bliss and God knew how many other exotics.

These guys were going for the arsenal.

In a world where power was the key, this had to be the pie of pies.

CHAPTER EIGHT

A CONTRACTION

Bolan stopped at the first public telephone and worked a combination to Hal Brognola. "It's time to regroup," he told him. "Send everything to Holloman. Do it quick and keep a low profile. That is, a *very* low profile. How soon can you be here?"

"Sounds heavy," Brognola said.

"Heavier than you may believe," Bolan warned him.

"You don't want to say it on the phone."

"No."

The fed sighed and said, "I can be airborne in ten minutes. You want everything, eh?"

"All you've got, yeah. And, Hal—don't report your movements to anyone."

"I should sneak, eh?"

"You should, yeah."

"Okay. Your cruiser should just about be

touching down at Bliss at this moment. I'll divert it on."

"Do that. Tell her to bring it into town the minute—wait . . . is Holloman the only field that can handle that C-One Thirty-five?"

"I don't know about that," Brognola replied. "Something wrong with Holloman?"

"Maybe. How far is Fort Bliss by highway?"

"Eighty miles or so," the fed said. "You want her to roll it from there?"

"That would be best, yes. She should bring it on into town and wait for me at the junction of highways Seventy West and Fifty-four."

"Okay. What about me?"

"What's the flight time from there, Hal?"

"It's about six hundred miles, Striker. Say an hour and a half."

Bolan said, "That would put the two of you here at about the same time. Hit the floater when you arrive. We'll work out a meet."

"Good enough. Uh . . . can you give me a clue?"

"Remember the guy in Colorado? The presidential caper?"

"You mean the soldier?"

"The same," Bolan said. "And this one is shaping up to make the first one a damn tame game, James."

Brognola said, "Tally ho, I'm on my way," and hung up.

Bolan grinned soberly and called the Jordan apartment. Mary Valdez picked up on the second

58

ring. He told her, "This is the friend. Everything's off. Clear out of there. Right now. Do you have a good car?"

Her voice was quivering a bit as she replied, "Good enough. Why?"

"I want you to get in it and drive, far and fast. Don't stop anywhere you're known and, for damn sure, don't go home."

"I don't understand what you want me to do," she said breathlessly.

Bolan explained, "I want you to find a hole and crawl into it. At least several hours away from here. And don't come back until you *know* it's okay."

"How will I know that?"

"Just read the newspapers," he replied.

"You think I'm in danger?"

"I know damn well you are," he told her.

"Well, so are you," she said nervously. "Two men are here waiting to see you."

"Waiting where?"

"They're parked right outside. They came to the apartment and asked for you. I mean, for Phil. I told them you'd gone out. But they're still out there, waiting in their car."

"What do you look like?" he asked her.

She described the Mafia torpedoes, "Bean" and "Nick."

"Driving a dusty station wagon?" Bolan inquired.

"That's right. You know who they are, then?"

"Yeah," Bolan said. "They're bad news. Okay.

Change of plans, friend. Don't try those guys. Slip out the other way. Leave your car and hoof it out of there. I'll pick you up. Go to the Seven-Eleven store on—"

She cried, "They're coming back!"

"Don't answer the door," he instructed her. "Bolt it and stall them as long as you can. Make them bust in, if they want in that bad. I'll be there in three minutes."

"Hurry!" she gasped, and hung up.

He would hurry, yeah. But he had a hell of a sick feeling in the gut. There was no figuring a logic where guys like those were concerned. They were capable of any rash action, and it had not taken the brief run-in with Marco Minotti to remind Bolan of that grim fact of Mafia life. But illogical action was not the only worry. It was just as possible that some aspect of that meeting with "the CIA guy" had stirred up something in Minotti's own guts. In that savage world, Bolan knew, instincts and hunches were the stuff of survival.

If Minotti's guts were quivering with Philip Jordan—then, yes, the guy would be following up on those quivers.

And if those torpedoes had been dispatched to deliver Jordan for a more prolonged parley, but found Mary Valdez instead, then Valdez could be seen as something of a gut-calmer herself. And that could be the beginning of the end for that lady.

Bolan made the dash to the Jordan apartment in less than three minutes.

But the end had already begun.

The picture window had been smashed, the door was standing ajar, and Mary Valdez was nowhere.

She was nowhere . . . right.

CHAPTER NINE

A QUICKENING

The Mafia wagon was parked in front of the northside house where the crew had stopped briefly earlier that morning. Bolan pulled in behind it, and affixed the silencer to the Beretta as he walked to the house. It was a ramshackle frame structure with peeling paint and advanced decay. The neighborhood was semiindustrial with several other homes in similar disrepair sharing the block with a junkyard and a trucking terminal.

Not a living thing was in sight or sound except a raggedy dog, which came groveling toward Bolan from an adjacent vacant lot. The dog changed his mind about Bolan when it came within a few feet, whimpering and turning tail in quick retreat.

The ancient porch had a rolling surface and uncertain foundation. Bolan took it in a single stride and paused for a quick sniff at the door. He could hear conversation in there, someone laughing.

The knob turned easily to his touch; he pushed the door open and stepped inside.

Mary Valdez was seated on a filthy, ragged couch. Her blouse was slightly torn and the hair a bit mussed, but she seemed okay—if you could discount primal terror.

There was no other furniture in the room except for a card table littered with beer can empties and overflowing ash trays.

Bean was leaning against a far wall, talking to someone on the phone, his back to Bolan.

Another guy whom Bolan did not recognize stood in the open doorway to another room, talking and laughing it up with someone in that other room, a beer in one hand and a cigarette in the other. He saw Bolan coming in and immediately raised the beer can in greeting. "Hi, CIA," he said nastily. Then he saw the Beretta and just froze there with the beer in salute.

Bean tossed a quick look over his shoulder, alerted by the greeting, then said into the phone, "He's here," and hung it up.

He, too, noted the ominously tipped Beretta in the second look. "Relax," he said with a glazed smile. "The chick's okay. We just wanted to get your attention."

"Congratulations," said Bolan, "you got it." And he blew Bean away with a chug and a sigh

The guy in the other doorway hastily emptied both hands, trying to stand erect and spring hardware at the one instant. The Beretta beat him on both counts, the quietly whispering round punching him in a sprawl into the other room.

Bolan reached that doorway just a step behind the bullet to find Nick in flight toward the back door. The room was a kitchen—or had been, once—now strewn with litter from an overturned card table, which had served as support for a hot plate and other small appliances. Also a Styrofoam cooler was overturned and disgorging ice and beer cans, which were rolling about the rough floor and creating a little problem for the fleeing hood.

The guy had a pistol in hand and a beer can underfoot as he crashed into the back door. He came around muttering foul words and trying to line into a shot at Bolan, but again the Beretta snorted first. The sighing round splattered into the soft underside of his chin and blasted on through the crown of the skull, carrying jellies and squirting fluids through the exit. The remains toppled back toward the center of the small room and came to final rest amidst the other trash.

Mary had come unstuck from the couch and was moving nervously about the middle of the living room as though confined within an invisible cage. Bolan asked her, "Just three of them?"

She jerked her head in mute affirmation, luminous eyes devouring him.

"You okay?"

Another jerk of the head and a fluttering of the eyes was the response to that.

"Okay enough to drive a car?"

She tried her voice, then, and found it—weak but serviceable. "I—I guess so. My God! You play *rough!*"

"I try to," he told her. "Do you have money?"

"I . . . my purse . . . at Phil's. Should I go back for it? Or I could go to the bank."

Bolan pulled five hundreds from his war chest and handed them to her. "Take Phil's car. Stop nowhere. Just hit the road and keep going until you're running out of gas."

"I can't take this!" she protested, trying to give back the money.

"Sure you can. It belongs to nobody." He showed her a sober smile. "Enemy money, liberated. It spends fine against them, though. Use it with my blessings. Now beat it."

She threw her arms about him and whispered, "Who *are* you?"

He gave her a quick squeeze as he said, "I'm the guy telling you to go . . . go . . . *go.*"

She disengaged rather reluctantly from the embrace, paused at the door to flash him a confused smile, then ran to the car.

Bolan watched her away, then turned back to the business at hand. He stripped the bodies of personal items and searched the house, but found very little to add to his understanding.

The guys carried New York ID, which was no surprise, and the house was very obviously a temporary camp with a recent beginning. And all the signs were for a short stay. Which maybe said enough, in a negative sense.

He backed the station wagon to the porch and loaded the bodies, carefully covering them with blankets.

Then he went back into the house and used the phone to locate Jack Grimaldi.

"I need some wings," he told his pal, the pilot.

"When and where?" was the ready response.

"I guess what I really need is a chopper," Bolan said. "Think you could pick one up locally?"

"Way ahead of you," said Grimaldi, rather smugly. "The only local chopper available for hire today is down for maintenance."

Bolan chuckled soberly and fed him the punch line. "But?"

"But I found one in El Paso. They ferried it up an hour ago. She's now serviced and ready."

"And people wonder why I love you so," Bolan replied drily.

"What people?" Grimaldi asked defensively.

Bolan chuckled and said, "I'll meet you at your motel in ten minutes."

"Okay. I'll call the airport and make it ready for a quick git."

Which was why Mack Bolan loved the guy so. They'd had a terrible beginning, yeah. But Grimaldi had made a tremendously significant contribution to Bolan's war effort. The guy could fly anything that moved through the air. And he had excellent combat credentials.

Bolan left the phone off the hook, got into the station wagon, and took his cargo of corpses away from there.

He did not wish for those bodies to be discovered right away. The pace of the day was quickening and he wanted to be riding the crest of that wave. With a little help, it could become a tidal wave—a cleansing wave.

Both the warwagon and Brognola's hotshot federal force should now be converging on the trouble spot.

Within about an hour, yes, all the actors would be upon the stage.

But the tide was quickening and Bolan could feel the waters rising all about him. He had to keep on top, a little out front, and in full command of the situation.

And Grimaldi's wings were little more than a forlorn reach for that position. At the moment, though, Bolan had only the faintest hope that those wings could keep pace.

If they couldn't keep the pace . . . then the only alternative would be to try to cool it down a bit.

And that could be a hell of a perilous alternative.

CHAPTER TEN

QUESTION OF THRUST

Roughly 4,000 square miles of New Mexico's land mass is given over to the White Sands Missile Range. The restricted zone is an irregular rectangle one hundred miles long by forty miles wide in its extremes. You could put the states of Delaware and Rhode Island in there and still have room to accommodate New York City and Philadelphia.

The terrain is a geologist's delight, including within its boundaries several mountain ranges, alkali flats, lava beds, sandy deserts, and soaring peaks.

Adjoining its southern perimeter is the Fort Bliss Military Reservation, another huge government area that extends south into Texas to El Paso and also juts east and north of the missile range to within a few miles of Alamogordo.

The two areas considered together, as one,

present an irregular perimeter of more than 400 miles encompassing some of the most jumbled landscape to grace this planet. In places it looks more like moonscape than landscape.

U.S. Highway 54 from El Paso splits the Bliss reservation up the middle, leaving it finally behind when less than fifteen miles south of Alamogordo, then runs north from Alamogordo along the eastern periphery of the White Sands range.

U.S. 70/82 traverses the southern region of the missile range, cutting a diagonal line between Las Cruces and Alamogordo and providing access, also, to the White Sands National Monument, a dazzling preserve of more than 200 square miles of white gypsum sand dunes, which is actually enclosed within the larger reservation of the missile range.

Holloman AFB is also situated just off this highway a few miles west of Alamogordo. The Missile Test Center, the actual "facility" at White Sands, sits in the southwest corner of the range just east of Las Cruces, some sixty miles from Alamogordo.

Immediately north and east of Alamogordo are the Mescalero Apache Indian Reservation and numerous winter sports areas with peaks in the 9,000- to 10,000-foot range; Sierra Blanca, just inside the Mescalero north boundary, soars to 12,000 feet.

This, taken together, was the war zone as presented to the tactical mind of Mack Bolan.

It was a humbling presentation.

A full army division could not be deployed in any effective hunt and kill operation in such a zone.

As for the Los Alamos question, the nuclear research laboratories were in the far northern part of the state, fully 200 air miles from Alamogordo. Bolan had to draw an operational line somewhere. Clearly, Los Alamos lay far beyond that line. He would have to hope and trust—at least for the moment—that a total victory within the established war zone would negate whatever treachery might lay beyond.

The problem at hand, here and now, was to delineate as clearly as possible both the size and the thrust of the enemy force.

And that was going to be a hell of a problem.

"That's restricted air space, you know," Grimaldi informed him. "There's no flight deck whatever. You can't fly over at any altitude."

Bolan was studying the aeronautical chart of the area. He said, "Harrelson is operating in there, Jack. Maybe he's kluging the system, passing as a bona-fide operational force. But I know damn well he's in there. His camp is up near Tularosa Peak, and that's inside the range."

"*Just* inside," Grimaldi grunted, craning his head for a better view. "The way you've lined it out, there, that camp could be just outside."

"Whatever," Bolan said, "the guy has combat capability and I doubt very much that he's contemplating a strike at the Apaches." He drew a small circle on the chart, then added spokelike radiation lines extending beyond the circle. "His instrumentation is approximately here. Please note, that's almost precisely at mid-range. He can monitor anything moving through that restricted zone."

"Or control it, maybe," the pilot observed.

"That's the scariest part, yeah," Bolan agreed.

"You think he's planning on capturing some birds in flight?"

Bolan shook his head and said, "I don't know, Jack. Sounds too wild, doesn't it? How do you harness a bird in flight? And bring it down intact? What about the warhead?"

"I guess you'd have to know if you were talking about free flight or controlled flight," Grimaldi said. "A free flight bird is no different than an artillery shell . . . or a bullet. You couldn't handle anything like that. But a controlled . . ."

Bolan said, "Suppose the bird is carrying a dummy warhead. You're testing controls only. Do you have to crash-land the damn thing or can you bring it down where you want it, softly?"

Grimaldi smiled as he replied, "You know the answer to that, Sarge."

Bolan said, "Sure. Chute recovery. Standard procedure. But if you wanted to steal one, that way, then you'd have to confuse mission control and work out a way to snatch it from under their noses. And you'd sure want to get more than one."

"Why?"

"Input output, Jack. Too much expenditure for too little gained. You couldn't even show that force from the proceeds of a single bird."

"Unless someone just wanted one to learn its secrets," Grimaldi suggested. "And they were willing to pay anything for those secrets."

Bolan sighed and said, "Maybe. But I believe there's more involved here than snatching a bird or two. What do you remember about White Sands, Jack?"

The pilot scratched his head and thought about it for a moment. Then he replied, "Just gossip, here and there. I heard something once about some tests on nuke systems. Los Alamos used to do some testing here. But I think that's all been outlawed now. I mean, you know, battlefield nukes. Artillery and light rocketry. I attended a class once in, uh—oh, toward the end—a class in developing weaponry. They were talking about nuclear warheads weighing less than a hundred pounds. For battlefield use, you know. They got, uh, some of that stuff deployed in NATO. They got, uh, artillery as light as One-Oh-Fives that are classified as nukes."

"I've seen them, yeah," Bolan said. "But I wonder if they test that stuff here at White Sands."

"I guess you could find out," the pilot said.

"I guess I'd better, yeah," Bolan muttered. "Something like that could be a dandy prize in the Mideast, couldn't it. Or in Africa. Or wherever blood flows between minor powers."

Grimaldi whistled softly and commented, "Wouldn't that be something, now? Can't you picture a freak like Big Daddy Idi Amin with nukes?"

Bolan growled, "I'd rather not."

"Well, you don't think these guys would really try for something like that. Do you? Nukes? Proliferating all over the damned world with all these third and fourth rate powers? Couldn't you see something like that injected into the Mideast situation? Boom goes the damned oil reserves, pal. Some of the nutties are already shooting down airliners with ground-to-air missiles. Give nukes to the radicals and you're going to see the whole world in flames. And that's exactly what they want, isn't it? They want the world in chaos so they can rebuild it the way they want it."

"It'd never get rebuilt by those guys," Bolan said quietly. "They're not the building kind."

"Look at Lebanon," Grimaldi said angrily. "Those crazy people destroyed their own country. And it was the most advanced country in the area."

Bolan said, "Yeah."

"Look at the fruitcakes in Italy . . . and Germany, France—hell, even in Ireland. God, those people have got no feeling for civilization at all. Their only God is politics. It scares hell out of me, Sarge."

Bolan said, "Yeah."

"You think this guy Harrelson would really go along with people like that? You saying the mob

73

don't care? You saying they'll do anything for a price? Even if it means . . . even if . . ."

After a moment, Bolan said, "Yeah."

Grimaldi pulled the car into the airport and parked it with a heavy sigh. He said, "I don't think I like the look on your face, Sarge. You're thinking of doing something really wild, aren't you? You've got some kind of a damn crazy stunt in mind, haven't you?"

Bolan cleared his throat, lit a cigarette, gave his friend a sad look, and said, "Yeah."

CHAPTER ELEVEN

FROM THE BLUE

They followed Route 54 north, maintaining a few thousand feet above the terrain, then circled back at Tularosa for a due south approach along the edge of the restricted zone.

Tularosa Peak now lay due west, just inside the zone.

Bolan growled into the headset, "Look at the wires on that peak."

The pilot took a look and replied, "Seems like standard telemetry gear, Sarge."

Bolan said, "It would have to. But I guess it could be authentic. Some things around here have to be."

"Sure. The whole area is bristling with that stuff. Where's that camp?"

That "camp" was damned hard to spot from the air. The collection of adobe huts in the lower valley pointed the way, though, and a flash of sunlight reflecting from some polished surface provided the fix.

"See that?" Bolan asked.

"Yeah. Is that the spot?"

"Has to be," Bolan grunted. "We circled a bit to the south before dropping into—there!—that's it at twelve o'clock!"

"Perfect," Grimaldi commented admiringly. "Whoever picked that spot—one degree either way and you'd never see it. Shee-it, I see the pad. You got no horizontal approach into that joint, buddy."

Bolan said, "It's hard to see from this angle but there's a—circle east, Jack."

The little 'copter heeled over and slid gently toward Route 54. The pilot was peering over his shoulder when he commented, "You can see the fenceline from this angle. They're just outside . . . practically on it. See it?"

"I see it, yeah," Bolan replied. "I'm still betting the instrumentation atop the peak is theirs, though." He was remembering a similar installation in the mountains above Los Angeles. And various things were coming together in his mind. He sighed, scratched at his chin, and said, "It's a go from my seat, Jack. But it's up to you. If you don't like the looks . . ."

"Your seat won't get there without mine, guy," Grimaldi replied with a worried smile. "How do you read the chances?"

Bolan locked eyes with his friend for a moment before saying, "The only chance we're going to have, buddy, is the chance we make for our-selves."

"I counted two gunships on that pad," Grimaldi said quietly.

"And there could be a dozen more within quick-reaction strike range," Bolan told him.

"Uh huh. So it all depends on a quick in and a quick out."

Bolan said, "It all depends on you, pal."

The pilot took a deep breath and said, "Okay. I'm game."

They were looping back northward, now. The adobe huts were directly below. Two vehicles were on the dusty road, heading out.

"Your way," Bolan said. "Go."

"There's only one way," the gutsy pilot re-sponded. He had been studying the terrain and now evidently had his approach fixed in the mind. "Hang on," he warned, and immediately altered the pitch of the rotor for fast descent.

The sensation in Bolan's belly was one of fall-ing in a runaway elevator. They fell for what seemed to be several thousand feet before the motion took on a noticeable horizontal attitude—and now Bolan could see the people on the ground in the adobe area. They were Indians—or appeared to be—and all in view were female. Some of them were shading their eyes and looking into the sky toward the "falling" aircraft—but then all that flashed past and Bolan realized that Grimaldi had executed a 180 during that descent and they were now sliding along the backtrack and angling into the buttes, at about 200 feet over the deck.

He could see the zigzag canyon through which he had earlier entered the stronghold and the present point of view confirmed the earlier feeling that the inner basin was considerably higher than the outer one.

Grimaldi was an absolute master of the rotary wing. The entire approach maneuver had consumed a mere few seconds; suddenly they were above the inner basin and settling quickly onto the operations pad alongside the Hueys.

Bolan growled, "Neat, neat."

"You've got to buy me at least a minute, guy," the pilot reminded him.

"I'd guess you already bought it," Bolan replied. He had the hatch open and was climbing out. Nothing in his vision field was yet moving inside that camp. He stepped out from beneath the whirling blades and took several paces toward the trailers, then halted and knelt to the ground as though to tie a shoelace.

Behind him, the rotors of the rented helicopter continued to churn the air in a neutral idle.

A guy in fatigues emerged from a trailer far downrange, shielding his eyes and staring toward the pad for a moment before moving back inside.

Behind Bolan, the deeper rumble of Bell Cobra power began to grow and quickly eclipse the churnings of the little bubbletop.

Bolan stood up and lit a cigarette, hunching

against the turbulence from the whirling blades and cupping his hands to shield the flame.

A jeep appeared from around the corner of a trailer, making its leisurely way toward the pad.

A guy in khakis hurtled out of another trailer to shout some anguished command to the man in the jeep.

The jeep stood on its nose and waited while the man in khaki sprinted toward it.

Bolan casually flipped his spent match into the air and walked back toward the whirling blades.

Grimaldi had the Huey firing smoothly and already beginning to rise off the pad. Bolan climbed aboard and they lifted away.

The jeep was directly below, now. Thompson was standing up in there and waving both hands in a frantic effort to call the chopper back.

But that chopper was not going back.

Bits and pieces from it, yeah . . . Bolan would gladly send that back. He was, in fact, already preparing to do so.

There was some kind of commotion outside. The soldier kept throwing these quick glances at the window, only giving about half of his attention to where it belonged. And Minotti was getting sick of this shit.

"Hey, I'm talking to you!" he growled.

"And I'm listening," said the stiff-ass.

"Well, what the hell is going on out there!"

The guy tossed Minotti a go-to-hell look as he

got up and marched to the window. That son-of-a-bitch marched everywhere he went. Minotti could almost hear drums beating and martial music every time that guy made a move. And he was sick of that shit, too. Still . . . you had to feel something for this guy. He was hard as nails, a big guy with a cast-iron jaw and not a damn soft spot on him—no soft spots between the ears, either. If the guy could only unbend a little, now and then. Did he always have to be on parade?

Minotti stayed where he sat and looked the guy up and down, wondering what the hell. "What is it?" he asked him, softening the voice just a bit.

"Helicopter," Harrelson said quietly, thoughtfully. "Incoming. Not one of ours."

"Oh," Minotti said, looking at his watch for no conscious reason.

The stiff-ass was at parade rest or something, standing there with the feet spread and hands clasped behind him, gazing out the little window of the trailer. He needed a swagger stick, Minotti decided. That would cap the whole thing off.

Suddenly Harrelson moved toward the door and tossed a single word to explain it all. "Jordan."

Minotti knew a sudden irritation. And he knew, now, why he'd instinctively looked at his watch. The boys must have blown it. They were supposed to. . . . If the son-of-a-bitch . . . Bean said he was *there*. Now Harrelson was saying he was *here*.

Well, there was going to be a hell of a scene, probably.

But, after all, who was bankrolling this damn. . . ?

Minotti surged to his feet and followed the soldier to the door. The guy went out to stand on the little porch, leaving the door open. The chopper pad was about a football field away. Minotti could see a figure emerge from the background of machinery, then drop to one knee.

Harrelson stepped back inside and told the radio guy to send a jeep to pick up Jordan.

Minotti growled, "Why don't you send 'im a fuckin' limousine. What? He can't walk a few hundred feet?"

The hardass muttered something about "courtesies" and returned to his desk.

Minotti just stood there in the center of the trailer, deciding on a little hard for himself. He yelled at Harrelson, "Courtesies my ass! You know how much goddam loot we got invested in this goddam thing already? Forget Colorado! I'm not talking about Colorado, although I could! I'm talking about right now! You know how much?"

The damn guy was a Southerner. His talk was a cross between buttermilk *you-all* and West Point *gesundheit*. And you knew when he was getting pissed because some of the *gesundheit* got left behind and it was almost entirely *you-all*. The buttermilk drawl told Minotti, "I can give it to you in fractions of cents, hoss, if you really want it. If you don't—what's this thing you've got for Jordan?"

"He gives me the goddam creeps," Minotti muttered. "Listen, I got a right to check out a guy that makes me feel that way."

"He didn't affect your people in New York that way," Harrelson pointed out calmly. "This has been his show from the very beginning. You know that. Why this eleventh hour freeze? Is it the interrogation? He learned that routine from your own people, so—"

"Aw, bullshit!" Minotti exploded. "It's got nothing to do with that. And let's get something straight right here and now! I *am* the people in New York! What I say goes!"

Harrelson stretched back in his chair as he replied, "So that's the way the ball has bounced. I've been wondering about that command structure. Since Marinello—"

"Hey, don't say that name in my presence!" Minotti stormed.

The guy was looking sort of amused and that just angered the Mafia boss all the more. He went over and kicked the guy's desk and yelled, "And I'm not throwing no switch for this so-called accelerated schedule until I feel better about that fuckin' guy! You put that in your fuckin' buttermilk and drink it!"

But he'd lost his audience again.

All that rage within the trailer could not now compete with the sudden hullabaloo outside.

Harrelson reached the door in three long strides

and was outside before Minotti could open his mouth to order him back. He yelled, *"Hey!"* and ran after him.

But the ironpants had taken no more than a couple of steps beyond that door. He had an army forty-five in his paw and was whirling about to shout something to the radio guy inside the trailer. Minotti collided with that whirl and both of them sprawled to the ground.

Meanwhile over at the pad one of those big gunships was taking off. The little chopper, which had brought Jordan in, was still sitting there with its engine churning but nobody in it.

The radio guy was now standing in the door of the trailer. Harrelson yelled at him from all fours, "Who's the idiot in the Cobra?"

The guy yelled back, "It's not an authorized liftoff, sir! Those ships are on ground secure!"

"I know that!" Harrelson raged. "Call 'im down, dammit!"

The radio guy disappeared back inside.

Thompson was out there cutting donuts in the jeep.

And stiff-ass Harrelson was damn sure fit to be tied.

Minotti found the entire scene hugely pleasing, although he was a bit disturbed by the confusion himself. But it was a kick to see these guys with their asses in their hands, for a change.

He said to Harrelson, "You're a little bit fucked up, aren't you?"

Then the scene focused a bit in his mind.

He snarled, "Where's that guy Jordan?"

Harrelson replied, very stiffly, "That guy Jordan is, I believe, in the Cobra."

There was a perverse pleasure in that, even though the captain's mood was more than a little disquieting.

Minotti was saying, "Well, that's just—" when the scene focused again.

The Cobra was almost directly above them now, maybe a couple hundred feet in the air.

Something flashed from the side of it, something bright and hot looking, then something else—or maybe the same thing—zipped away and flew a hot beeline to one of the big equipment rigs at the far side of the camp.

The big equipment rig was instantly engulfed in flames and the whole goddam place shook with the *kaboom* that came away from there.

Minotti screamed, *"Is he crazy?"*

But the stiff-ass was not talking, now, neither in *gesundheit* or *you-all*.

He had Minotti by the arm and he was pulling him along in a fast retreat to the cliffs.

Sirens were going off, all around the place, and suddenly the whole camp was alive with running men and pandemonium.

This was crazy! It was just crazy! What the hell was going on?

That crazy CIA guy was shooting the place up!

An electronically amplified voice was wafting across the compound to compete with all the other sounds, endlessly repeating, *"Situation Blue, Situation Blue, Situation . . ."*

And it was that, okay.

It was a hell of a blue situation.

CHAPTER TWELVE

FRIENDS AND FOES

The craft was a Bell Huey Cobra, white-glove clean and fully outfitted with rocket pods and fifty-caliber machine guns.

"This is old home week," Grimaldi grunted as he lifted her away.

Bolan went straight to the fifty-caliber mount to check out that impressive weapon. "Cross the fingers," he muttered into the intercom.

Grimaldi was chuckling. "They're trying to raise us on the radio," he reported. "Aw, hell, they're mad at us."

It was at that moment that Bolan spotted Harrelson.

The two had not met eyeball to eyeball in Colorado, so it had been a long time—but it was instant recognition, nevertheless.

And it could have been yesterday that they

were eyeing each other over a Montagnard camp-fire along the Ho Chi Minh trail; the guy had changed not a quiver.

For one fleeting instant, now, their eyes met and locked at a distance of perhaps a hundred feet or so . . . and it was one of those electric moments. Bolan realized once again that it is not the face of a man that carried identity, but the soul itself, projected through the eyes. Because there was an instantaneous mutual recognition in that meeting of eyes. Frank Harrelson had never before seen that face in the chopper . . . but he knew who was looking at him . . . and Bolan knew that he knew.

During that moment, Jack Grimaldi exultantly reported, "She's hot! I've got a firing go!"

Bolan broke the eye contact with the frozen man on the ground to yell back, "Let's see something burn, then!"

A Two-Two whizzer leapt away immediately and streaked to a meeting with a heavy equipment van. The whole target erupted into a fire-storm and the shock wave from that hit staggered even the big Cobra.

Grimaldi was some kind of damn guy. He'd flown more combat missions in gunships just like this one than most guys would want to think about and he had a string of decorations as long as the arm. He could fly anything that could ride the atmosphere and he had nerves like piano wires, with guts to match. Yet he'd been unable to find satisfactory employment in a nation weary of no-win warfare and embarrassed with its returning warriors.

What a goddamn waste!

But he was not being wasted now. He was coaxing that fabulous weapons system into a performance her designers had only dreamed about, and one quick look at the guy was all it took to know that here was a man in his own element and in full command of it.

Bolan's weapon was a "flex fifty," which merely meant that it could be targeted and fired independently of the attitude of the aircraft—but there were limitations to that, of course. Beyond those limitations, the gunner must depend upon the quick cooperation of the pilot to establish a firing line into a hot spot. And one of those hot spots had presented itself as a quick echo of that missile hit. A squad of uniformed men with assault rifles had tumbled into view for a hot response to the emergency.

Hundreds of fire missions had conditioned Grimaldi for the proper reaction. He knew these ships and knew their fire parameters. He must have known, too, that Bolan's fifty was about ten depression degrees shy of the hot spot. The chopper rolled and dipped just like a conditioned reflex and Bolan's big fifty cut through that rifle squad like a scythe in wheat.

Only it was not wheat, of course, but the flesh and bone of men Mack Bolan had once regarded as comrades.

And there was no joy there, no.

He turned the fifty onto the machines at the operations pad and coolly dismantled the enemy's flight capability from that camp, concentrating upon mechanical effects, which would disable but not destroy.

The little rented bubbletop sent her idling blades windmilling into a nearby trailer. The tail rotor of the grounded Cobra dropped away, taking a sizeable piece of the tail assembly with it. The three smaller choppers took their disabilities via shattered cockpits and mangled landing gear.

Two fuel tankers, off to the side, blew columns of fire heavenward.

Meanwhile Grimaldi had sent some more firebirds streaking through the New Mexico atmosphere to wreak havoc on the installations there. Three large vans and two instrumentation trailers were in flames when Bolan gave the signal for breakaway.

The Cobra cocked her rotors for quick git and the whole hellish scene down there slipped away in a twinkling as Grimaldi expertly swung away in a terrain-hugging withdrawal. Not until they were swooping once more over the adobe huts did he send her stretching for altitude.

"Well done," Bolan breathed into the intercom. And he was not just blowing smoke at the guy. It had been spectacularly done. The wrist chronometer showed an elapsed time of just under two minutes from touchdown to breakaway.

The pilot growled, "Guess I'm getting too old for this. How do *you* feel?"

"I feel terrible," Bolan admitted.

But someone else, he knew, was feeling a hell of a lot worse. And that was the whole object of warfare.

"You never get used to this stuff," said the veteran pilot.

Bolan said, "Ummm."

"What?"

"You wouldn't want to get used to it, would you?" Bolan asked quietly.

"God no."

"But . . ."

"But what?"

"Ask me how many men I've killed today, Jack."

"How many men have you killed today, Sarge?"

"Not," Bolan replied quietly, "nearly enough."

Minotti began breathing again and raised himself to hands and knees. Harrelson helped him to his feet and the two of them stood like statues at the edge of the chaos.

"What the hell happened?" the *Mafioso* mumbled.

Harrelson raised both arms in front of him, then let them fall limply to his sides. "Your eyes are as good as mine," he replied in a choked voice.

The eyes were sort of hard to believe, though. Just a minute ago this place had been an impressive and smoothly functioning military encampment with gobs of exotic equipment worth millions and millions of dollars. Now it was . . .

The whole place seemed to be on fire. And nobody seemed to be doing anything much about that. Columns of smoke were rising high into the sky—visible, probably, in Alamogordo.

Thompson drove up in a jeep and stood up in it to make his report to Harrelson from above the windshield. "We have six dead and two seriously wounded. All of the aircraft are disabled and will require extensive repairs. We lost the fuel tankers. We lost two power vans, the electronics lab, the communications facility. All, total loss. We do still have limited radio capability."

Harrelson may have looked a bit stunned but he was not the kind to fold up and cry over his losses. "Okay, let's move the rest of it out, on the double. We'll consolidate at Point Echo. Recover your casualties and move them with you. Activate Contingency Bravo."

"Aye, sir."

But the guy was still standing there. Harrelson snapped, "So what are you waiting for? I said on the double!"

"It was Doctor Jordan, Cappy."

Minotti growled, "I knew that son of a—"

"It was Bolan," Harrelson declared coldly.

"No, sir. I saw him clearly. It was—"

"You saw what he wanted you to see!" Harrelson snarled. "The guy in that Cobra was *not* Phil Jordan!"

Minotti burped and said, "Oh hell, that's it, that's why I couldn't stomach the guy."

Thompson was not backing off, but he had a new look in his eye as he argued, "It was the same man who was here earlier, who verified the Rickert analysis, who stood and talked with Mr. Minotti and me."

"Then it was Bolan all the way," Harrelson quietly insisted.

That did it for Thompson. He said, "On the double, aye," and sent the jeep plunging back into the chaos.

"So now what?" Minotti inquired despairingly.

"So now the impossible merely becomes a bit more difficult," Harrelson replied casually. "Don't worry about it, Banker. You ain't lost nothing yet, hoss."

Brave words, sure.

But what the hell . . . the guy had already done the impossible, hadn't he?

"You'll just work a little harder," Minotti quietly suggested.

"And a little faster," Harrelson said.

"But especially a little harder," said the *Capo Mafioso*. "I want that guy's head, Harrelson. I want to take it home with me."

"You will," said the trooper, "have to take it away from me, first, mister."

Which was a lot of shit. But at least they both had the same idea in mind.

* * *

92

The Huey Bell Cobra was on station high above the strike zone, hovering at almost the limit of her service ceiling. Both occupants were observing the activities below through powerful binoculars.

Grimaldi muttered, "Well, I'll be damned. You were right. They're moving it west, into the restricted area."

"Only way to go," Bolan replied quietly. "That's where their pay dirt is, Jack."

"Do I keep them in sight?"

"That's the only reason we're here," Bolan told him.

"They'll pull us right into the security zone."

So be it, then.

Bolan suggested, "Turn on your IFF transponder. I'll bet you the whole arsenal that it's set to the proper response."

"I'll bet you're right," Grimaldi said with a sober smile.

Bolan was right, all right. And that was easily the scariest damn part of it all.

CHAPTER THIRTEEN

THE VARIABLE

They got it together in a motel near Alamogordo —and it was quite a gathering. Brognola's rolling command ships and Bolan's cruiser took up much of the truck parking at the rear; the federal force occupied half of the ground-level rooms.

"Don't worry about the visibility," Brognola quietly told Bolan. "The management thinks we're a news crew, out here to cover some exercises." He grinned. "They even gave us a special rate."

April Rose had given Bolan a bit of low-keyed hell during the early moments of reunion—including some well-phrased thoughts on "abandoned brides" and "damn short honeymoons"— though of course there had been neither marriage nor honeymoon, except in the broadest possible sense, and she had obviously intended a half-humorous expose of her anxieties.

But she had not taken her eyes off him since

that moment—hell, she was fairly drinking him down through the eyes—and he was finding the warm attention just a bit uncomfortable.

He told her, "Cut that out."

She smiled knowingly, but replied, "Cut what out?"

"You know what," he growled. "And with your boss looking on, at that."

"Don't worry about it," she said. "I intend to be entirely professional while the occasion demands it. But I also want you to know what's in store for you, soldier, when that occasion goes away."

He told her, "I already got the message. So—"

"Let it sink in, then, and let it bring you through the day in one piece. Don't go flinging yourself around like there's no tomorrow."

Brognola stepped back into the room and asked, "What's that about tomorrow?"

April lightly replied, "I was just telling him to save some for tomorrow."

Brognola sniffed at that. "Tell it to the wind, April." He unrolled a detail map of the White Sands Missile Range and spread it on the table in front of Bolan. "This the one?"

"That's the one," Bolan said. He spent a few seconds marking the chart with a red pencil, then explained: "These are the known hot spots. There could be more . . . or they could change rapidly. I don't have a good feel at all for the size or full intent of this force." He drew an X through the Tularosa Peak encampment. "This *was* Mission

Central, I'm sure of that. As of about an hour ago," he drew a dotted line to another encirclement, "they moved it to here. And it didn't take them long to do it."

"Why did they move it?"

Bolan smiled. "We sort of encouraged them to."

"Uh huh." Brognola pulled up a chair and sat down. "Who is *we?*"

"Maybe we shouldn't get into that."

"Maybe we should. Maybe I need to know who's in the damn game."

Bolan stared at his hands for a moment, then took a scrap of paper and wrote a name on it. He handed the information to Brognola and said, "I guess it's time to get this guy on your list, at that. He's been with me since Glass Bay, on and off."

Brognola was staring at the scrap of paper. "This is the guy who . . . ?" He cleared his throat, placed the paper in an ash tray, and put a match to it. "Nashville?"

Bolan nodded his head. "And many others." He winked. "Seattle. Texas. And he's been a steady source of intelligence. I wouldn't have come this far without him. Put him on your endangered species list, huh?"

"I'll do that," the head fed replied drily. "Where is he now?"

Bolan smiled. "He's babysitting a captured gunship."

Brognola's eyes flared. "What?"

Bolan nodded affirmation and explained, "A Huey. Full armament. The latest and greatest configuration available. All the newest communications gear, black boxes, firepower enough to raze a small city like Alamogordo . . . all of it."

"Where the hell did you get it?" Brognola asked quietly.

Bolan tapped the X on the White Sands chart. "They had two of them, plus several small scoutships. We borrowed one Huey and disabled the other. Couldn't bring myself to destroy it. Which worked out okay because they left it behind when they withdrew. I suggest you get some people up there damn quick, though, to take custody of that stuff. Also there's a small chopper belongs to a flying service in El Paso. Jack is worried about it." He grinned. "It's checked out to him and I think he's a bit concerned about the insurance coverage."

"I'll take care of it, sure," Brognola growled. "How many other gunships would you guess they have?"

Bolan said, "I believe you could determine that better than I could. Just find out how many have been sent to this area through official channels over the past few weeks. Look to Fort Bliss, especially."

"You think the guy is working the Pentagon faucets again, eh?"

"I'm sure he is," Bolan replied. "Maybe I didn't make myself clear. This Huey, Hal, is a legitimate U.S. Army gunship. It's a Cobra and it's fully equipped with all the secret gear. You can't just go out and buy those things."

Brognola went to the door to pass some instructions to the brain trust in the next room, then he returned to perch on the desk facing Bolan. That good face was pulled into worried lines as he inquired, "Where does Jordan fit into all this?"

"They call him Architect," Bolan explained. "That's a code name. I believe the whole thing was his brain child. With his contacts and knowledge of DOD routine—well, it would take someone like that to pull this thing."

Brognola muttered, "I guess I better make it a full alert. But God I hate to . . ."

Bolan quietly told him, "Don't let me second-guess you, Hal. It's your responsibility . . . and I'm sure you're better equipped than I am to . . . uh, well . . ."

"Out with it," the fed growled. "Don't pussyfoot me, dammit."

Bolan grinned soberly and continued, "I believe there's a *force* at work here, sure . . . but I'm not so sure it's a force in the way we usually think of it. I, uh, I'd sure as hell like to see a computer study on recent personnel changes in this area. I, uh . . ."

Brognola said, "You think they've stacked the deck."

"Something like that, yes. I can't get this Jordan guy out of my thinking. I know that type of mind and I know how it operates. Devious . . .

devious as hell. Nothing so blatant and chancy as a paramilitary force running around out here in the desert under the noses of the legitimate military establishment. Yet, they seem to be doing exactly that. One chance meeting, Hal—hell, one wrong twitch of the eyes and . . . these military people around here are not idiots. The whole thing could blow sky high over a small breach of military courtesy. And that would be the smallest of worries."

"So what are you saying?"

Bolan relaxed into his chair and lit a cigarette. April was giving him the warm-worried look. Brognola was waiting for a bomb. Bolan felt like he was throwing one as he said, "There are a lot of disgruntled people in the military today, Hal."

Brognola grumpily said, "So?"

"High people. And not just in the military, but throughout government service."

"You're talking about treason, you know."

"Call it what you like," Bolan said. "I'm talking about human nature and the imperfectibility of man. I'm talking about people who grow cynical and corrupted because of the way power is routinely abused without penalty in this country —hell, in every country—and I'm talking about a plot to steal some of the most sophisticated weapons ever devised by the military mind. So don't try to tell me that a guy with Harrelson's brains and background would barge in here with some harebrained scheme to do battle with the United States Army—on their own ground, yet."

"You're still pussyfooting me," Brognola complained.

"I'm trying to elaborate the problem, Hal. And I am simply telling you that Jordan, Harrelson and Company have been given some sort of assurances that they will not encounter any significant resistance out there."

Brognola's eyes fluttered as he said, "Okay. Say it's true, then. So we need to know how high and how wide goes the treason, before I go pushing any alert buttons. I guess that's what you're saying."

Bolan growled, "That's about it, yeah."

"And what if we cannot make such a determination?"

"I don't believe we can," Bolan replied. "Not in time. They're talking about an acceleration. I guess that means a deviation of sorts from the original plan, whatever that was. I do know that they are worried about the implications of the California hit, yesterday. The problem with every great plan is that you cannot always cover every variable. And, yes, I believe they're worried. They went to a great deal of time and trouble to grab Charlie Rickert and sweat his bones for intelligence. And now . . ."

"And now?"

"Well, now they know that I'm onto them. I believe they will be making their move very quickly. I mean like right away, today."

"You're saying they *know* that Mack Bolan has joined the game."

Bolan nodded. "That's right. I wanted them to know."

"Why?"

"Because I hope to make them play my game instead of their own."

"What will that accomplish? In real terms, I mean."

"In real terms," Bolan replied, "they could defeat themselves. They'll move at my pace, not theirs. They'll make mistakes."

"You hope."

"Nobody's that perfect, Hal. Something like this calls for precision drill. Like a football team. Any quarterback can complete ten of ten passes if all he has to do is stand back there and throw. Put a couple of linebackers blitzing his butt on every throw, though, and he'll gratefully settle for five of ten."

Brognola sighed and splayed his fingers across the White Sands detail. "What you're saying, I take it, is that you want to do all the linebacking yourself?"

Bolan quietly replied, "That's it, yeah."

"Why?"

"Because we don't know who are the friends and who are the foes. They're all wearing the same colors. And I keep thinking of this guy Jordan. You say he was a think-tanker. I say okay, he's had a lot of time to brain-trust this one. You send for help, okay, but I'm saying you'll never know which side of the street that help will be coming from. And that help, when and if it gets here, will simply add to the confusion."

"That's your finding?"

"Yeah."

"You are absolutely sure."

"I'm sorry, yes, I am absolutely sure."

"Well, relax," Brognola said, sighing, "so am I."

Bolan smiled grimly and said, "You're a couple of steps in front of me, aren't you?"

Brognola took a deep breath and said, "Yeah. I wanted your inputs before they could be tainted by . . ." He opened a leather case and produced a thin stack of computer print-outs. "Here's the DOD file on Jordan. I told you he was psych-war specialist and tank thinker. Well, he was more than that. At times, a hell of a lot more. As he got older, though, he was used almost exclusively as a thinker. He was what they call in the tanks a scenarist. The guy wrote fiction. But fiction with a particular edge. The point is to dream up every conceivable threat to the national security. The scenario is a step-by-step detail of how a particular threat could unfold. The challenge, then, is to beat the scenario with another—how to reduce the risk of the threat-scenario, how to respond in case the threat-scenario should become a reality."

"I've heard of the routine," Bolan murmured.

"It's standard Pentagon routine, sure. There are people doing that all the time. Must be a bunch of paranoid guys haunting that place. I suppose that right this minute, in some scenario being developed and played in a Pentagon think tank, eighty or ninety million Americans are lying dead in the streets as a result of a sneak nuclear attack. Washington is probably in flames, maybe the whole White House staff has been assassinated. But the attack did not come from Russia or China—as you might expect—but from India or South Africa, maybe even England or France. These are nightmares, see—nightmares—deliberately induced so that our planners can systemize some methodical reaction to anything that could conceivably develop. Another scenario could be playing right next door, which has the entire eastern seaboard writhing under nerve gas . . . from Cuba."

April wrinkled her nose and commented, "I'll take the first case, thanks."

Brognola went on, "I'm just trying to show you where Philip Jordan is coming from. All scenarios do not, of course, deal with overt military actions. Or they don't even have to have a military context. There are political scenarios, religious scenarios, visitors from outer space scenarios. Hell, Hollywood never came up with anything better."

April said, "I had some small exposure to that during computer training. We worked with some of the models and antimodels."

"What's an antimodel?" Brognola growled.

She explained, "The scenario emerges from the think tank as a computer model. Then they have to play those models off against possible solutions, which in turn produces contingency models, statistical evalutions, and various other planning devices. The antimodel is the solution to the model."

Brognola said, "That's computer talk for plot and counterplot."

"Okay, I'm with you," Bolan said quietly.

Brognola sighed heavily and replied, "No, I'd guess that you're a bit ahead of me. That printout—which is top secret, by the way—that printout includes a brief summary of Jordan's scenarios, which were developed during his last few months at DOD. You will find one in there, near the end, which is titled *Infiltration and Capture of White Sands Missile Test Center,* et al, *by Small Terrorist Group: The Seizure of Sophisticated American Arms for Indiscriminate Application in Political Causes.*"

Bolan said, "That's a mouthful. How'd it play?"

"It played too damned well, I guess," Brognola replied soberly. "It became an obsession for the guy. Nobody could beat the model. Jordan kept playing with it, long after he'd been repeatedly ordered to drop it and go on to other problems. I guess his superior figured the scenario was just too far out to warrant that much attention. Anyway, like I said, Jordan apparently became obsessed with the damned thing. The obsession finally lost him his job. He had CIA connections. Talked a section chief into taking him on covertly to continue work on the White Sands problem. That's a bit kinky, of course. CIA has no legitimate interrest in domestic problems. I guess there was question enough regarding overseas inputs to at least

104

make it an iffy project for covert concern. Nobody at CIA will admit to knowing anything about what the guy was doing, although he was certainly on the payroll for nearly two years. He was not fired, incidentally. He resigned. Less than a month ago."

Bolan sighed and said, "With his model intact."

"You got it, pal. And now we are looking at the reality, not the model."

April inquired, "Why couldn't anyone beat the model?"

Bolan suggested, "Because Jordan had devised an insoluble problem. The way he laid it out, there's no way to beat it."

"Which is precisely," Brognola pointed out, "what Striker has been telling us."

April said, "Then what. . . ?"

Brognola said, a bit wryly, "Well . . . Jordan did overlook one small variable. He left something out."

"What did he leave out?" she asked.

Brognola coughed delicately and flicked his eyes at Mack Bolan as he replied, "He left out Striker."

CHAPTER FOURTEEN

THE MODEL

There was little room for doubt that the Jordan scenario had become a self-fulfilling prophecy. It mattered little, now, what had motivated the guy. But it was impossible to not wonder about it.

April tended to feel a bit sorry for Jordan. She seemed to believe that his original motive had been only to prove that his scenario was a valid worry, that perhaps he became a bit unhinged and lost himself somewhere during the development of that proof.

Brognola pointed out, also, that Jordan's record prior to the White Sands incident had been impeccable.

And Bolan could not help thinking of the late William McCullough of Los Angeles and his flirtation with cannibals.

So it was entirely possible, of course, that April's sympathy was not entirely misplaced.

Maybe the guy had just lost control of the thing . . . or of himself.

Whatever, the computer summary of Jordan's "problem" left no doubt that the model had become a reality—with perhaps only a few insignificant modifications.

The scenario postulated a sensitively placed government executive who, for "immoral or political motivations," becomes allied with a terrorist or paramilitary organization. This executive is capable of breaching security apparatuses in such a way that "unfriendly agents" are able to quietly infiltrate a government facility "where sophisticated arms are deployed, stored, or routinely tested," there to seize control of those arms and transfer them out of the country before their loss is even discovered.

Such a plot would, of course, require some rather extended cooperation involving diverse elements of the military structure. They would need people with at least the basic technical skills to handle and transport the purloined weaponry. And they would need long-range transport aircraft, which could operate under a military guise and thus escape the country without incident.

The computer summary provided by Brognola did not go into deep detail, of course, but it did hint at a rather elaborate scenario. Apparently the "unfriendly agents" would be recruited from both ex-military men and those still serving. The force would be composed of "specialists and technicians of diverse types" as well as combat personnel and flight crews. Those not now actively serving in the armed forces would be "surreptitiously reactivated and their service records appropriately altered to accommodate reassignment to the target command."

What would then follow would be a systematic shuffling of personnel via the Pentagon's own apparatus: straight men out, crooked men in.

As simple as that.

It would not even be necessary to completely replace all of the straight personnel, but only those in particularly crucial positions. The fewer replaced, the tighter the plot.

Specialty groups—such as, perhaps, the bunch at Tularosa Peak—could be moved in en masse, under quasiofficial orders, as a temporary or special detachment—perhaps even under the cloak of a top-secret operation.

And, of course, there was always a horde of civilians moving through facilities such as the one at White Sands—employees of defense contractors, scientists and technicians, civil service people. Bolan thought vaguely of Mary Valdez in that connection, then tried to very quickly drop that lady from his mind.

He could only hope that she had taken his advice.

As for the White Sands scenario . . . it could work, sure. Its greatest strength was its apparent simplicity. Like all good tactical plans, though, the simplicity masked a highly elaborate and daring master concept.

Better yet, this one did not even require any wholesale corruption of the host system. One or two key men with special skills could successfully manipulate the machinery of government from some obscure post within the Pentagon—from, say, a position as computer programmer or personnel specialist.

Another one or two, well-placed within the security network, could neutralize any counter-movement by a suspicious official.

Simple, yes.

It was not difficult to see why this scenario had been deemed insoluble. No doubt it had also been branded as impractical by those who could not solve it.

Needless to say, those who had so judged the scenario were also guilty of having "left out" a vital factor from their judgment.

They had left out Doctor Philip Jordan.

And that had been a hell of an omission.

Because Jordan was, of course, the missing "key man"—the Architect.

And his was—yes, certainly—a self-fulfilling scenario.

CHAPTER FIFTEEN

TO WINDWARD

The situation, Bolan knew, was precisely the same as if an entire military command had suddenly gone berserk and decided to go into business for itself. Except that the present situation was a bit worse, because at least you could throw massive force against a berserk command and crush it. You could not do that here, in this situation—not unless you were willing to punish the innocent along with the guilty—and, of course, that was too harsh to even contemplate.

It was probably something less than five percent of the local troops who could be counted in the enemy column. Which, yeah, leaves much too many of the good guys with both feet in hell.

So the first and most ticklish task would be to define the enemy. And maybe the only way to do that would be to let them define themselves. Which was not quite as mystical as it sounded.

"Did you get those studies I requested this morning?" Bolan asked the head fed.

"It's still developing," Brognola replied, then tossed the ball to the lady. "April?"

She jerked her head in a curt nod and told Bolan, "We should have summary runs within about ten minutes. The query program covers a multitude of variables. I had to write it myself. Believe it or not, there is no master program which will systematically interrogate the various data pools related to this problem. You'll have to ask someone else in government why the tools of management are not being employed when they are so readily available. Perhaps it has something to do with bureaucratic competition, but I'm damned if—" She caught herself, smiled apologetically, and went on. "Sorry 'bout that. Guess I get preachy when I see this sort of thing."

Bolan said, gently, "You had to write the program. And you were about to say . . ."

"I just wanted to say that there is probably more stolen from this government than is ever actually used by or for government. The GSA is an absolute cesspool of incompetence and downright knavery. That means both waste and theft in wholesale lots. GSA could clean up their act and probably reduce the cost of government by twenty-five to fifty percent. And, listen, the people in this country can forget about Big Brother watching them. I doubt that anyone is watching anything. I'm not at all surprised that a smart operator can step in and make monkeys out of the

111

bureaucrats. Anyway, what I'm trying to say—there is no overviewing software. I had to create some. You did want a total picture?"

Bolan smiled and replied, "In a local sense, yes."

"Okay, I had to cover all the inflow—including such things as personnel, materiel, money, food, clothing, as well as a few that are not so obvious. I—"

Bolan asked, "Such as?"

She tossed her head and said, "Such as medical supplies, combat rations, test equipment, fuel, PX supplies, movies—"

Brognola arched his eyebrows to say, "Movies?"

"Motion pictures, sure. It provides a picture of on-facility entertainment requirements. That equates to personnel confined to the facility for extended periods. Same as PX supplies. Toothpaste, shaving cream, and the like."

Bolan said, "We're convinced. Go ahead."

"I try to balance all that in terms of outflow and/or accretion."

He asked, "Some general parameters?"

"The same," she replied. "That's how we determine certain anomalies which would not otherwise appear."

"Did you query comparative periods?"

She said, "That's part of the general overview, yes. But the periods compared, in an area such as this one, must be pertinent to specific activities. As opposed to periods of general inactivity. This is a test area, remember. Therefore there should occur a periodicity of inflow/outflow related directly to testing activities."

Bolan grinned at Brognola and remarked, "Damn, she's smart."

Brognola grinned back as he replied, "Pretty, too."

"I could resent the hell out of that," the lady said, "except I know that you're both only trying to be honest."

Brognola chuckled and said to Bolan, "I have a feeling I'm going to lose her to GSA."

"Cut it out," April requested good-naturedly. She touched Bolan's chin with a tiny fist and said, "I'll go and brood over the printers. Maybe I can hatch those summaries."

Bolan kissed the fist. She raised it to her lips and strode out of there.

Brognola was beaming. He said, "You guys are working out okay, eh?"

"Great, yeah," Bolan muttered. "Maybe too great. I can't afford that lady, Hal."

"Sure you can," said the fed. "You have a whole new life waiting just over the horizon. You can count it in sunsets, now. Three more after today. Just three more, pal."

Bolan growled, "Maybe. And maybe that horizon is no more than a cruel illusion. I'm beginning to wonder if I sold myself a bill of goods."

"Don't start thinking like that, Striker," Brognola said.

Bolan smiled at his friend and replied, "I appreciate the concern. Believe it. But, Hal . . ."

"Hell, don't say it."

"I have to say it. Look around. Look around you, right now, and tell me where you see a defeated mob."

"Either side of the street can be an illusion, you know," Brognola argued. "Don't start thinking of Harrelson and Jordan as organized crime figures. That's stretching it too far. Those guys are—"

"Chow," Bolan said.

"Huh?"

"Those guys are chow for the cannibals. Like McCullough."

Brognola sighed. "Maybe so. Okay. I won't bullshit you, guy. There does seem to be a resurgence. That's only natural. They are not going to lie down and die just because things have been going to hell for them. They're fighting back, sure. But I happen to believe that my department can handle that. Better than you, even. Because the game has changed. Thanks entirely to you, it has changed. You weakened them enough to give us our ins. We have ins everywhere now. We're all over those guys. Believe me, we can handle them. You asked me to look around. Now I'm asking you. Look around. Here's a problem that, quite honestly, I do not know how to handle. It's a military problem, dammit, and I don't believe the military can handle it. Do you agree?"

"I agree, sure."

"Okay. There are very similar problems occurring all over the world, right now, this minute."

"Hal, I—"

"Give me my say. I know how you feel about the mob. I feel the same way. But, Striker, there are far graver problems facing this country, this world. There's a new wind a'blowing. The thing that you are facing right now is precisely the *sort* of thing you *need* to be facing from now on, for as long as that wind continues to blow. Why? Because, dammit, you're the best there is, and because we cannot afford to field the second best to handle problems like these. Let me give you a sneak preview of what you're going to find in April's summaries."

Brognola paused to light a cigarette.

Bolan lit one from the same match. He released the smoke and said, "Sneak preview, eh? From your own pipeline?"

"That's where from, yeah. I've known it for weeks, although not . . ." he spread his hands to indicate the surrounding environment, ". . . not in this context. There has been a steady movement of sophisticated weapons systems into White Sands for the past three weeks. I mean everything from nukes to chemicals, the very latest and the very greatest in tactical warfare capability."

Bolan glanced toward the window and asked, "Under what pretext?"

"No pretext whatever. Strictly legitimate. A

115

scheduled event. There will be a demonstration for NATO field commanders, right here, on the day after tomorrow."

"Wrong," Bolan said quietly.

"Why wrong?"

"Because," Bolan replied, "by the day after tomorrow there will be nothing left with which to demonstrate." He put out the cigarette and ran a hand through his hair. "How much stuff, Hal?"

"Too damn much," Brognola said, "to end up in Algiers or Lebanon or wherever. Enough to ignite the whole damn Middle East. And when that region blows, buddy, we all blow with it."

"Do you have any inside information that would lead you to the conclusion that the stuff is destined for the Middle East?"

The fed shook his head. "Just a gut feeling. That's where the hottest emotions are. It's also where the dollars are. But wherever they end up, wherever they are used, it would be a shocker for the whole world. We'd have to write new manuals for diplomacy and international politics."

"You're saying nukes and chemicals."

"Right."

"Nerve gas, all that."

"All that, yeah."

Bolan made a harsh sound deep in the throat and lit another cigarette. "I thought there was a test moratorium on that stuff."

"There is. They'll be demonstrating the delivery systems, using dummy warheads. But the real warheads, plenty of them, will be on display."

116

"The new miniature stuff?"

"That's the kind, yeah."

"How would you price that stuff?" Bolan muttered.

"You can't price it," Brognola replied. "And if you're thinking in petrodollars, well hell, the sky's the limit. Those people can't acquire such weapons legitimately from any power at any price. The eastern powers are as scared of proliferation as we are—maybe more so."

"The mob is bankrolling this hit, you know," Bolan said quietly. "Frank Minotti's kid brother is right here on the scene."

"That would be Marco," Brognola said.

"Right. I guess he's the local mouth for New York."

"Wrong," said Brognola. "We're reading Marco as the new *boss* of New York. Well, almost. I guess he needs this one. It would cinch the spot for him."

Bolan said, "He can't have it, Hal."

"It isn't exactly a new situation for the boys, you know," Brognola reminded him. "They were running arms before they started running booze. Except now I guess it's a hell of a lot more profitable."

Bolan growled, "Better than drugs or casinos, sure. I guess they're probably dreaming of becoming the arms brokers of the third world."

"It's the new wind," Brognola said, sighing.

"Well, I guess we'd just better turn on a fan," Bolan muttered.

"You got one handy, pal?"

"If I don't have, I'll build one."

"You'd better build it damn quick," the fed said.

"We could lose this one both ways, you know," Bolan told him.

"What do you mean?"

Bolan held up his cigarette and gazed at the glowing tip. "If we lose," he said quietly, "both problems get entirely out of hand."

"Which both problems are we talking about now?"

"That resurgence you mentioned. They win this one, Hal, and it could be much more than a resurgence. It could be a rebirth."

"Okay. Maybe."

"You know damned well I'm right."

"Okay, you're right. What's that other problem?"

"Military," Bolan quietly replied. "If all the nations begin hurling nukes around, pal, you don't have a military problem. What you have, then, is a military resolution. And that's what we've all been trying to avoid. Isn't it?"

The head fed shivered and went to the door. He turned back to pinch at his cheek and say, "Okay, it's yours. I'll give you until nightfall before I push the panic button. What kind of support will you need?"

Bolan asked, "Do you have a hot loop with Washington?"

"Direct to the man, yeah."

"He's been alerted?"

"Only in a very general sense. He knows that something is going down. He does not know what it is."

Bolan sighed. "You'd better tell him, Hal."

"I fully intend to. Right now."

"Tell him also, then, the importance of tight secrecy. Jordan will have placed wires everywhere. These people are not playing around with satellite communications systems just for the fun of it. Tell him about our suspicions concerning the California connection."

Brognola was wearing a perplexed frown. He said, "He'll have to set up a fail-safe contingency, Striker."

Bolan replied, "Sure, but just make sure he understands that it must be done very quietly. As extra-military as possible."

"Okay. Anything else?"

"I'll need some orders cut for two men, White House mission status with full overrides. Make me a colonel and Jack a major. We'll need full ID and credentials."

"That's easy. What else?"

"We'll need the proper clothing. Uh, combat outfits. Jack weighs about one-fifty. He's five-ten and properly proportioned. Shoe size . . . probably an eight. Head . . . well, say seven and a fourth. That's all."

"That's all the support?"

"For now, yes. Keep your force on their toes and ready to move. Monitor all the standard military radio channels and keep scanners on everything else."

April pushed through the door at that moment, bearing a heavy stack of computer reads. "It's started," she announced gaily.

"All I want right now is personnel," Bolan growled. "Put a crew to analyzing the other stuff. I'll want the results on a piece of paper I can carry in my pocket."

She blinked at him and said, "Do we get all of ten minutes to carry out those orders, sir?"

He told her, "I'll settle for that, yes."

"Nuts!" she cried. "You're getting ready to fling yourself again, aren't you!"

Bolan met Brognola's worried gaze above the girl's head. "With all possible haste," he quietly told the fed.

Brognola sighed and went on out.

April deposited the computer runs on the table and turned brooding eyes to the man. "Aren't you?" she said harshly.

He took her hand, and squeezed it, and told her, "But not at windmills this time, April."

"What?"

"This time," he said quietly, "I have to *be* the windmill."

CHAPTER SIXTEEN

GETTING IN

A sergeant with MP markings on his uniform saluted smartly and shouted to make himself heard above the dying revolutions of the rotors: "Begging the colonel's pardon, sir, you can't land that thing here, sir!"

Bolan returned the salute and replied, "You're wrong, sergeant, it was a perfect landing. Take me to your C.O."

Grimaldi had set the Huey down on the headquarters lawn. The time was midafternoon and apparently quite a lot was going on in the administration area of the test center. Foot traffic, both military and civilian, in the immediate vicinity was heavy, and the parking areas were choked with vehicles.

The MP was caught between command imperatives, but it was very obvious that the big "colonel" in the neat desert fatigues embodied a command that would not be denied. The guy snapped another salute, this one to the debarking pilot of the Huey, and resignedly led the visitors away.

It was a gleamingly modern brick building with a comfortable reception lobby bearing mementoes and symbols of the historical significance of these proving grounds. Some special tables were being set up in an area marked "Press Orientation" and the lobby was swarming with human activity—in preparation, no doubt, for the upcoming special event. In the midst of all that activity a rather calm-looking guy wearing captain's bars was busily setting up a desk bearing the placard *Public Information Officer*.

The PIO smiled at Bolan and Bolan smiled back. "Getting it together, Captain?" he inquired pleasantly.

"It's getting there, sir," the PIO replied.

Bolan felt right at home. The colonel's insignia on his tunic was about the only thing out of place. And he was finding that as natural as his sergeant's stripes had ever been.

They swept on past there and along a broad hallway with offices opening to either side. At the end were large double doors bearing the insignia of DARCOM, the Development and Research Command of the U.S. Army. In small detail appeared the name of the commanding general at White Sands along with further information that this was a facility of the Test and Evaluation Command at Aberdeen.

Bolan and Grimaldi were taken into the C.O.'s outer office and deposited there in the custody of an aide, one Major Paul Whitney.

The MP quickly withdrew.

Whitney was a pleasant enough guy, relaxed and casually dressed in shirtsleeves. "I take it that's your chopper outside the general's window," he said, slightly amused by it all.

Bolan handed the aide a sealed red envelope as he told him, "This is White House hot so don't lose it between here and the general's desk."

The smile slowly evaporated as Whitney turned the envelope over in his hands a couple of times. He said, "Right. Right, sir," and quickly excused himself.

He was back about thirty seconds later, holding the door open to the inner offices. Bolan and Grimaldi stepped inside and the aide went on out, closing the door behind him.

The guy at the desk was youngish for a general with a tough cut to the jaw and very intelligent eyes. Bolan gave him a casual salute and moved straight into a handshake. "The President sends his regards, General," he soberly greeted the C.O.

"It seems that he's sending more than that," said the general. "What's this all about, Colonel Phoenix?"

Bolan introduced Grimaldi as Major Conti, then replied, "I am not authorized to reveal anything beyond the contents of that envelope, sir."

"The hell you're not!" the guy exploded. "Do you know what's *in* this envelope?"

"Only in the most general sense, sir," Bolan replied respectfully.

"It has the *general* effect, Colonel, of relieving me of my command!"

"No, sir—by your leave, General—that is not the intent of the orders. It has been firmly impressed upon me that I am not to interfere with your command in any way that is not absolutely essential to the conduct of my mission."

"And what is that mission?"

"I would have to refer that question to the White House, sir."

"Good enough!" the general snapped. "Wait outside!"

The visitors gracefully retreated to the outer office. The aide offered them coffee, which both accepted. A pretty secretary went into a small alcove and quickly produced the offering. Bolan sipped his and said quietly to the aide, over his cup, "The general's a bit on edge."

"Why not?" the guy replied pleasantly. "This is the biggest thing we've had in years. You have any idea how many things can go wrong? We're going to have all the big brass of Europe within our humble walls tomorrow."

"It should be pretty much routine by now," Grimaldi observed quietly.

Whitney nodded his head at that as he replied, "We run about a thousand tests a year, sure. But that's not the problem. The problem is courtesies and protocol. This isn't exactly the Presidio, you know. What do you do with twenty foreign generals? Not to mention all their staff people, the press, and all that. We're hard put just to bunk them all."

"Seems like a nice enough place," Grimaldi said, discreetly probing for information. "You guys have a regular oasis out here. Trees and grass, flowers. I don't see why there should be any problem."

"It's nice enough, sure," the guy shot back. "For us. But, listen, some of these buildings have been here since nineteen forty-five. They've got terminal desert rot. The better part of it all is the family housing area. We only have thirteen hundred military people assigned to this reservation, so that makes for a damned small town. Most of the other space is taken up by the four thousand civilian employees and two thousand contractor personnel. Of course, they don't live on site. They just work here."

"You've got that many contractors, eh?" Grimaldi said.

"Well, the army only administers this range, you know. Everybody uses it, all the services, all the defense contractors—even a lot of foreign governments. Hell, DARCOM is just a pimple on the tit. But the pimple has to run the whole body."

"Yeah, well, you've got a problem there okay," Grimaldi said, smiling at the guy with innocent good nature.

Bolan commented, "But surely you have more than thirteen hundred men in this command."

"Look, that's all we have," insisted the aide.

"How many of those are involved in range security?" Bolan asked casually.

"Is that why you're here?"

"Something like that," Bolan vaguely replied.

A bit of caution was creeping into Whitney's demeanor. He leaned forward to say, "Our range security is very good. It's *all* controlled access, you know, and very strictly controlled. Our boys do a good job."

Bolan murmured, "I'm sure they do."

"Bet your ass they do, sir."

"Is it beefed up for the coming event?"

"Beefed up? I just told you, our security is very good."

Bolan smiled and reached for a cigarette. The aide lit it for him. Bolan settled back into the chair and said, "But you've taken no special precautions on behalf of the visiting brass?"

The guy was becoming decidedly nervous, now. He looked from Bolan to Grimaldi and back to Bolan again as he replied, "We're more worried about their comfort than their security. These aren't visiting heads of state, you know. They're soldiers. Is there something . . . is that why . . . what's this all about, Colonel?"

Bolan smiled again and told him, "Your general will tell you all about it, I'm sure. After he's spoken to the White House."

The general's aide turned a bit pale at the mouth. He gave Grimaldi a wounded look and said to him, "What I have been saying to you gentlemen is entirely off the record. If you people are checking out our—"

Bolan shut that off with a wave of the hand. He said, "Relax, Major. Nothing is going into any record. You don't see any white gloves on our hands, do you?"

Whitney replied, "No, sir. I'm sorry. I only meant . . ."

He never did tell them what he only meant. Bolan and Grimaldi finished their coffee in silence.

The secretary glanced their way from time to time and self-consciously fiddled with various things on her desk. Obviously she had nothing else to do, at the moment. The general's aide gazed out the window and squeezed his hands together.

He was a nice enough guy. Bolan said, "Don't sweat it, Major. Our visit has nothing whatever to do with range administration. We're checking in here only as a courtesy. After your general has cleared us, we'll be on our way and you won't even know we're here."

The guy showed him a tentative smile as he said, "Thanks. I needed that. It has been a hell of a sweat for the past three weeks."

A buzzer on his desk sounded at that moment and he quickly went to the C.O.'s office. He returned a moment later and handed the red envelope to Bolan. "The general extends his welcome and hospitality," he reported quietly. "I am to provide all your needs, whatever they may be. I'll notify the provost marshal and the security detachment of your carte blanche status on the range. We can greatly facilitate all that if you will just accompany me to the security office. It will take just a moment to make up the badges, which will clear you to all areas of the range."

Bolan was on his feet. He said, "That will be fine, thanks."

"How about billeting? Will you be staying. . . ?"

Bolan waved the idea away. "You have problems enough with billeting," he told the guy. "We won't be here long enough to rest the head, anyway."

The aide seemed very relieved about that.

"Follow me, please," he said, and led them toward the keys to the kingdom.

But it was not to be all that cut and dried.

The security office was in a smaller, more modest structure within a comfortable walk from headquarters.

The general's aide was ushering the visitors into that building when Bolan came eye to eye with one Mary Valdez.

The lady was wearing a crisp khaki blouse with knife-pleated slacks and she paled to an absolute white at sight of Bolan.

He thought she had fainted and moved quickly forward to grab her.

But it was just a stagger. The lady caught herself and struggled against the attentions of the tall colonel in desert fatigues.

"I—I'm okay," she gasped.

The general's aide had not missed any of that. He said, "What the hell is it, Mary?"

Color was flooding back into that pretty face, going to the opposite extreme. "I'm sorry," she apologized in an embarrassed near-whisper, speaking to the aide. "I thought for a minute he was Charlie."

That obviously meant something to the aide. And he was suddenly very understanding and solicitous. "You okay now?" he asked her.

She said, "Sure. Really, I'm fine. Are you here to see me?"

"Not exactly," Whitney replied. "But why not? Why not the best, eh? Will you take care of our friends for me?"

"What do they need?"

"Range clearance, all areas."

"On your say-so?"

"General's orders," he advised her.

The lady looked at Bolan, then, for the first time since that initial surprising confrontation. "Okay," she said spritely. "Step into my office, Colonel?"

The aide told him, "I'll leave you in Mary's hands, Colonel. Oh, uh, I'm sorry, this is Mary Valdez. She's chief of the security section. If, uh, you need anything more, you'll know where to find me."

Bolan nodded agreement with that. The guy excused himself and departed.

Bolan and Grimaldi moved on into the security

office. The lady was standing at a desk near the window, her back to the door.

Bolan quietly inquired, "Who's Charlie?"

"Someone I once knew, a very good friend, a very long time ago," she replied without turning around. "He's dead."

Grimaldi murmured, "I'm sorry."

"Take a chair, gentlemen," she said quietly, ignoring Grimaldi's condolences. "I'll be right with you."

Bolan said, "It's okay, friend. This is another friend—Major Conti, Mary Valdez. He knows. It's okay."

She turned to face them, then, with a half-smile working at those ripe lips. "Knows what?" she asked.

"He's working with me on this problem." Bolan handed her the red envelope with White House seal.

She took the envelope, sat down, read the contents twice around, then said, "I see."

Then she fell apart. Her hands were shaking visibly as she returned the presidential orders. Tears oozed from her eyes and down those glistening copper cheeks. "It's true, then," she whispered. "Phil is really dead."

Grimaldi looked as though someone had just slapped him.

Bolan told the lady, "You're damned lucky that you are not. Why didn't you take my advice?"

She opened a drawer of the desk, withdrew a

sheath of hundred dollar bills, and pushed them across the desk at Bolan.

"Why, Mary?" he persisted.

"I don't need your money. Thanks just the same."

He said it again. "Why?"

"I went to the captain, instead," she replied tearily.

"*Which* captain?"

"I think you know which captain," she said. "And I think he knows you, too. He tells me that your name is Mack Bolan."

Grimaldi sighed heavily and muttered, "Well, shit."

And, yeah, that's what they were in, probably —and, no doubt, very deeply.

CHAPTER SEVENTEEN

GAMES

The small office at White Sands was enveloped in a long, electrically charged silence before Bolan asked the lady, "Do you know who Mack Bolan is?"

"Who doesn't?" she replied woodenly, looking at the window instead of at him. "He's a murderer. A crazy. One of the most wanted criminals in the country."

"And you're saying that is what I am?" he asked gently.

She looked at him, then, and said, "You seem to have the knack of being whomever you decide to be. I'll bet there are times when even *you* don't know who you are. Like Phil. I thought, at first, back there at the apartment, that you were just another of his kinky playmates . . . and it was just another game."

Bolan asked her, "What kind of kinky? What kind of games?"

She said, "Never mind. Obviously I was wrong. I knew it wasn't a game when you stepped into that old shack and started shooting everybody in sight."

"I didn't shoot you, Mary," he reminded her.

"So you didn't. Thanks. But for what?"

He shrugged and replied, "I thought it mattered. To you, I mean. It sure mattered to me."

"Why?"

He smiled at her and said, "We're friends."

She shuddered at that. "Some friends I get. Boy. Sometimes I can hardly believe my good fortune."

He said, "I'm sorry you feel that way. I thought something special had happened between us. I trusted you. Still do."

She gazed at him for a long moment, then said in an agonizing little voice, "I just wish I knew who you *are*."

He asked her, "Why would Mack Bolan be sitting here in the White Sands security office posing as Colonel John Phoenix?"

"Which one are you?" she asked, peering at him through new tears.

"Who is this captain you mentioned?"

"You answer mine first."

"I'm Mack Bolan," he told her.

Grimaldi grunted and shifted his weight about in the chair, started to say something, changed his mind.

The lady had blinked her eyes rapidly at Bolan, then averted her gaze. After a moment, she said, "You sure have a way of keeping people off balance."

"You owe me an answer," he reminded her. "I gave you mine."

That pretty face was torn between a smile and a frown as she said, "You're Mack Bolan, eh? *The* Mack Bolan."

He winked at her and replied, "What are mere names between friends, friend?"

She said, "Go to hell," but still entertained mixed emotions, almost giggling. Either she was becoming hysterical or her sense of humor was asserting itself . . . black humor, maybe.

The whole bizarre scene was beginning to get to Grimaldi, obviously. He growled, "Jesus Christ! What's going on here?"

"Give us a moment," Bolan requested. He flicked a glance at the door.

Grimaldi got up with a sigh and stepped outside, closing the door firmly behind him.

Bolan offered the lady a cigarette, which she declined. He lit one, blew smoke at the ceiling, and very soberly told her, "I killed Phil, Mary."

She gave him a ragged look and said, "Dammit, don't . . ."

"I'm not playing you. Please believe that. I think you're a hell of a lady. I like you. And I can't believe that you're a traitor."

That jerked her around. She replied, very deliberately, "I am not a traitor. Do not ever suggest

134

that I am or ever could be. A fool, maybe—an idiot, a dumb Indian broad who can't separate sexual fantasy from love and reality, but you are not to even hint that I may be a traitor to my country. My skin may not be exactly the same color as yours, but let me assure you—"

Bolan snapped, "Dammit, cut that out!"

She murmured, "Go to hell, friend."

"That could be where we'll all end up," he bit back, "but meanwhile we have this little problem called life in the upper world. Now, dammit, I need your help!"

She glared at him for a moment, then dropped the eyes and said, "You killed Phil, huh?"

"Yes."

"Why?"

"Because he was playing nasty little games with living human flesh. He was burning out eyeballs and peeling away skin and doing things to genitals I'd blush to describe to you."

"You're insane!" she gasped.

"No, Phil was the crazy one. He spent too many years playing with insane scenarios and developing too many heinous ways to destroy the world. And I believe he got trapped in all that, I believe he lost himself in it—a desperate, mad soul who felt the need to destroy the world in order to prove something to it. I put a bullet between Phil's eyes, Mary, because I caught him with a living man's intestines in his hands and I simply could not think of anything better to do with the monster. I'm sorry if that caused you

135

pain or brought a sense of loss to your life, but I want you to believe me when I tell you that you lost nothing worthwhile there, kid—not a damn thing."

Something was stirring in those tortured eyes. She said, "You really are Mack Bolan."

He replied, "Call me what pleases you. But, dammit, help me save this day."

"What do I have to do?"

"Just be as honest with me as I've been with you."

"No games?"

"Please no games," he said with a solemn smile.

Another silence descended.

Bolan finished his cigarette and put it out.

Grimaldi rapped lightly at the door with his fingertips. Bolan told him, "A moment, Jack," and peered insistently at the girl.

She sighed and asked, "What can I tell you?"

"You can tell me everything you know about Phil and, uh, this captain."

Grimaldi tapped again and called through the door, "Time is getting short, Colonel."

The lady slumped and rested a weary head on arms stretched across the desk. "Okay, friend," she whispered. "Let him in. I'm going to tell a story to shock your toes. But remember . . . I am *not* a traitor."

No, she was not a traitor. Nor even a dumb broad. She was simply a lady who'd had a problem with sexual fantasies. But not her own.

136

* * *

The Cobra lifted away, and Grimaldi uttered his first whole words since they had left the security office. "Did you buy all of that?" he growled.

"I bought it, yeah," Bolan replied quietly.

He bought it, sure, because there was nothing else to do with a story so sad, so bizarre, so damned humanly tragic. Mary had met Phil Jordan shortly after she came to work at the test center, during one of his frequent visits to the facility. She was a graduate of the University of New Mexico at Albuquerque, but her roots were sunk deeply into the earth around Alamogordo and she'd considered herself highly fortunate to find a good job at the test center.

The families of both mother and father traced their own roots in this land to a time when it all belonged to Mexico. Her father was of Mexican descent and owned a small parcel of land, which had survived in the family from a large Spanish grant. Her mother was a Mescalero Apache, and her mother's mother had been born on the reservation near Alamogordo.

None of that had any particular relevance to the present state of affairs except as a setting for a Mexican-Indian girl of humble beginnings who'd managed to struggle through four years of higher education, land an excellent job with a career appointment in U.S. government service, and meet the "man of her dreams" —an erudite intellectual, highly placed in that same government service.

It had developed into more of a nightmare, though, than a dream come true.

Mary had known for a long time that her relationship with Phil Jordan was going nowhere. It was almost entirely a sexual relationship: "If you could call it sex. A lot of it wasn't. It was . . . I don't know what to call it, but it was not sex. Not for me."

The guy apparently had some rather kinky hang-ups. But she'd thought she loved him. And she'd hung on to the hope that she would one day bring him around somehow to a normal relationship.

Perhaps that was why she had accepted such indignities from the guy for such a damned long time.

"The first thing he pulled on me like that," she told Bolan and Grimaldi, "I thought I would die of shame. And I thought that he had to have a terribly low opinion of me to . . . to expect me to go along with anything like that. But it got easier as time went on. And I blame only myself. Phil never even tried to rationalize any of it to me, never asked for understanding. I was the one who rationalized, tried to explain . . . to myself."

What she had tried to explain to herself would no doubt have provided ripe meat for a team of psychiatrists.

On their very first intimate date the guy took her to a motel, made love to her all the way through the precoital embrace, then backed away at the crucial moment and brought in another guy from outside—a total stranger to Mary—to stand in for him while he looked on.

A stunt like that could, yeah, make a girl feel a bit unsure of herself—and of her man.

"I knew he had a problem," she explained. "My mistake was in thinking I could help him overcome it."

But things never got much better for Mary Valdez. There was infrequent moments when she and Jordan "got it on very nicely, almost normally," but always preceded by some degrading, humiliating stunt for Mary.

"He started bringing the captain around about a year ago. That's all he ever called him—the captain. I never heard the man's name until today. But we'd played games many times before, involving military titles. Once he dressed me in a full uniform—an officer's uniform with general's stars. He ripped the crotch out of the trousers and wanted me to bend over. Well, you know what he wanted to do. I talked him into just pretending he was doing it and we got it on pretty well that time."

Dismal, yeah, sad and tragic. Mary Valdez's "honesty session" would have played better from a psychiatrist's couch or confessional booth. But even that side of the story had given Bolan a valuable insight into the problems of the moment —and the rest of it, that part involving "the captain," was extremely valuable.

It was interesting, for example, to know that Jordan and Harrelson had been close acquaintances for at least a year.

It was interesting, also, to learn of some of the joint interests shared by those two during the course of that year.

"So where do we go from here?" Grimaldi asked "the colonel" when they had lifted away from the headquarters building.

Bolan replied, "Think you have those recognition codes pretty well doped out?"

The pilot had spent the early afternoon shaking down that Cobra and discerning her secrets. He told Bolan, "I'm pretty sure, yeah."

"Sure enough to try that range camp in the northern zone of Bliss?"

Grimaldi shrugged and replied, "What do we have to lose but our lives? You're buying it as a hot spot, eh?"

Bolan was buying that, yes.

Mary Valdez had spent a weekend there, precisely three weekends earlier, as the "guest" of Harrelson and Jordan.

As the guest of both, yeah. And a whole damn company of horny troopers.

CHAPTER EIGHTEEN

GOING FOR IT

The Fort Bliss access to the White Sands range served primarily the army's air defense training command. A couple of range camps just south of the Sands provided launch facilities for ground-to-air missiles in conjunction with drone targets operating in the restricted airspace above White Sands. Those range camps were not continually operational, but saw occasional periods of inactivity between training missions.

According to the readout from April's computer summaries, the camps had been inactive for the past six weeks—and were to present date. So an anomaly had emerged from the study. Two batteries of ground-to-air missiles had been dispatched to the area ten days ago for "non-launch exercises" and were presumably still in the area, though there was no "read" for scheduled exercises or for personnel to conduct those exercises.

141

Several other interesting results had emerged from the studies, involving other areas of the White Sands Missile Range, but the Fort Bliss training camps were the nearest at hand, and also there now existed substantiating proof, of a sort, that something unusual was occurring at one of those camps.

So a look at Fort Bliss was a logical first step in the sequence. And it yielded the first blood of this potentially bloodsoaked afternoon.

A small clump of weathered buildings on the desert east of the Organ Moutains marked the spot—and again Bolan was struck by the "bandit camp" parallel with the Old West, though this time the stronghold was a small desert town and the outlaws carried thunderbirds in braces instead of six-guns on the thighs. A dozen or so men were visible within the encampment. Also a jeep, several weapons-carriers, and two of the huge transporters used as mobile launch platforms for ground-to-air missiles.

It was going to be a touchy situation. It had to be. Firstly, Harrelson's troops were certain to have been alerted to the attack at Tularosa Peak and to the missing Huey. All of the strongholds would most likely be sensitive to any visit from the air, and especially in a gunship.

Also it was at least an even bet that the word had gotten around concerning the presence of an important emissary from the east on a secret mission for the White House.

Either way it read for these guys at Bliss, it was not to be a duck-soup operation for Bolan's team.

"No radio contact," Grimaldi reported as they approached the camp. "They're playing it close."

Which right away ruled out a couple of options for the visiting team. "Get into PA range and hold," Bolan instructed his pal, the pilot.

"We'll be sitting ducks, you know," Grimaldi advised as he skidded the big bird into a hover at one hundred feet up, one hundred feet out.

Bolan growled, "Just keep the eyes open, Jack." He cut in the PA system and called to the ground. "Camp Strong. Flying Heart above. We're coming down to parley. Give us a sign."

He said to Grimaldi, "Hope you've got those signs doped right."

"Don't make any long range plans on that," the pilot replied nervously.

But they got their "sign" after a short delay: two quick flares from a Very pistol fired from the porch of a central building.

"I guess that's close enough," Grimaldi decided. "The card shows two circles as the proper response. I guess those circles could mean flares."

Bolan said, "Put her down, then. Do you see the set?"

"I see it, yeah."

The "set" was a triangulated fire team, two men each arranged at two, six, and ten o'clock around the edge of the campground. The guys were standing casually in relaxed attitudes, but each carried what appeared to be a Stoner 63A1 light machine gun and had drifted into that set position, which would allow maximum adjustment according to developing need.

The gunship settled gently and Grimaldi quickly powered-off to a ground-idle. He released his belt as he told Bolan, "Better let me take the point. They may like my looks better than yours. Besides, I never got along too well with those fifties."

Bolan had to accept that judgment. He replied, "Play it cool, Jack. And go with my cue."

"Right."

The remarkable guy grabbed a Stoner off a rack beside the hatch—a weapon identical to those awaiting him on the ground—and affixed a 150-round drum. He slung the machine gun from the shoulder, muzzle down, and went out to "parley" with the strongmen of Camp Strong.

That was a code name, of course. It was just one of those unhappy facts of warfare that they'd had to come in so close before they could make that identification. If the bogus soldiers had responded to the radio signal, the Cobra could have held away and smoked them neatly from a safe distance. The antiaircraft missiles on the transporters showed no signs of launch readiness and it was even doubtful that they could be employed at such close range. Those babes were radar-guided and could smoke a plane long before human senses could perceive it. With those birds nested away, though, it would have been a far neater operation from an airborne Huey.

But this was not an airborne gunship. She was on the ground inside a hostile camp and Bolan's old pal, the amazing flyman, was moving off alone into a den of predators.

And now Bolan knew how this good friend must have felt during those many anxious occasions when it had been Bolan out there afoot on savage turf while Grimaldi waited and watched.

Yeah. They, too, die a little who but wait and watch.

But Jack Grimaldi was not going to die even a little this time and Mack Bolan was not one to wait and watch beyond a crucial moment.

He was following with narrowed eye the progress of the choreography out there, willing with mind alone the movements a few degrees this way, a few degrees that, sucking in the breath of life as though somehow there would be none left to suck if one false step were made.

"Straight ahead, Jack . . . straight ahead," he muttered to himself—then, *"Okay, okay . . . there! Now!"*

Two people in dirty fatigues were moving forward to meet him as Grimaldi stepped from the shadow of the gunship. Both wore sergeant's stripes and had obviously been involved in some sort of mechanical chores very recently. Their hands were blackened with oil or grease, much of which had found its way onto the clothing.

145

These two also packed army forty-fives in military harness at the waist and the faces wore uncertain greetings.

Grimaldi moved on toward them with both hands plainly unencumbered and called forward, "Hey! You 'bout ready?"

Both "sergeants" came to a halt and one of them called back, "What's with the off-again, on-again bullshit? What is it this time?"

Grimaldi, also, halted and took a quick look around. The fire team was moving in, closing the encirclement—the two at six o'clock edging up toward oh-five-hundred to get a better alignment on Grimaldi past the tail of the Cobra. He called up, "We couldn't raise you on the radio. What's the matter?"

Other guys were moving into view, now, from the scattered buildings. This was obviously a technical crew primarily, not too heavy in the combat infantry department. All wore side-arms but the only real combat weapons in sight were the Stoners with the fire team. The other guys were all soiled and had sweated through their fatigues, disgruntled-looking and idly curious about the visitation.

The sergeant with greasy hands was shouting at Grimaldi, "One minute you say radio silence, the next you say you can't raise us. Are you people sure you know what we're doing?"

Grimaldi began moving slowly forward again, grinning and waving his hands against the noise from the idling rotors. Those boys on the fire teams were technical specialists, sure, who'd never learned the finer nuances of hellground tactics. They were folding in toward the middle, trying to get close enough to overhear the vocal exchanges through the other noise, their attention focused on the man on the ground instead of on that deadly Cobra.

Grimaldi had honed his hellground tactics to a survival art, thanks. And he knew what that formidable man left behind at the flex-fifty was waiting for, and hoping for, and praying for.

And, yes, it was as though the two minds were one. Grimaldi could feel the breath congealing in his lungs as the strike perimeter constricted. He had calculated the flex zone of the fifty and extrapolated from that his own zone of responsibility —and it was almost a subliminal quiver flashing between single-minded partners that set the thing in motion.

The Cobra's big fifty crackled through the rotor sounds and sent fire lacing into that east perimeter; at the same precise moment, Grimaldi flung himself into a whirling reach for Stoner power. His own little five-fifty-six was chattering into the upper circle like a stagger-step behind Bolan's fire, reaching for the zone beyond the flex and finding immediate meat.

The whole damned fire team was down and gone in the initial flash of the strike as that blazing partnership proved its promise.

The two sergeants in the greeting party died with greasy hands and full holsters, their chests

147

popped open and spraying life's own ruptured lubricants under the steel-jacketed impact of heavy bullets from a hot fifty.

The other guys were running and yelling in every direction—and it was so goddam easy, it was brutal.

The big magnificent warrior came charging out of the Cobra with a Stoner in his strong paws and a new drum of ammo for Grimaldi—and they went a'hunting . . . and took no prisoners.

It was not a time for prisoners.

At issue, after all, was not the value of individual human lives but the security and well-being of the entire human family.

So, no, it was not a time for prisoners.

And they took none.

CHAPTER NINETEEN

BIG FLY, LITTLE SKY

"Alice this is Striker on channel Bravo. Do you read?"

Brognola's good voice echoed back strongly on the special tactical net. "Alice here, Striker. Go."

"Strike your chart at coordinates Delta Four. That's a hot spot just gone cold."

"Got it, right, Delta Four. Anything there for me?"

"Yeah, a double nest of chicks on wheels awaiting bye-bye. You should make a point to get there first."

"We'll see to it," came the response. "Where away are you now?"

"We're headed for the big fly. A-OK here. Striker gone, off the channel."

Grimaldi announced through the intercom, "Ten more minutes to Holloman. What do you expect to find there?"

"Many wings," Bolan replied, "and big ones. They have to get this stuff out of here somehow and the sky is the only way to go."

"It will take some damned big planes," Grimaldi agreed. "And lots of them. Sounds kind of nutty to me."

"These things always sound nutty until they work," Bolan reminded him. A moment later, he added, "The transport angle is the whole game, Jack. It's one thing to waltz these weapons around White Sands. Something else quite again, though, to get them out of the country and tucked away somewhere beyond recovery.

"Still sounds nutty."

"Sure it does. So did the first hijack of an airliner. Things like that work *because* they're nutty. Nobody would think of it, until they do."

"Well, listen," Grimaldi said, "those birds back there at Camp Strong are tucked away for transport now. But they'd just got that way. Did you see the stuff in the operations shack?"

Bolan muttered, "I saw it, yeah."

"Damn right." A moment later: "They had delineated target sectors and the whole smash. I took some training with one of those outfits, once. And that wasn't there just for show, in case someone happened along. I think those guys had a fire mission. I think they'd planned on using those birds, right there."

Bolan replied, "Looked that way, yeah."

"Well, what do you think the mission was?"

150

"Some sort of diversion, maybe," Bolan mused. "Or a fail-safe of some kind. This thing has been planned to the final detail, Jack."

"Obviously," the pilot agreed. "So why were they preparing to withdraw from Camp Strong?"

"They've accelerated the schedule," Bolan explained. "So it could mean anything. Maybe the acceleration negated the Camp Strong mission. Or maybe they were just moving to a different camp. Maybe a fail-safe, to protect the air getaway. I don't know, Jack. I'm playing the ear, guy, just like forever."

The pilot grunted deep in his throat and turned his attention to the radio. He was getting a hit from Holloman Control.

Bolan relaxed in his seat and listened to the approach instructions with only a portion of his mind. There were many things yet to be considered and evaluated in this crazy caper concocted by a madman.

A very dangerous madman, yes.

And an insanely dangerous concoction.

Bolan walked into the Holloman operations office and took the place over. He served the red envelope on a rosy-cheeked captain, gave the guy a moment to gape at the contents, then ordered him, "Get your security honcho up here on the double."

The security chief took several minutes to get there. While they waited, Bolan paced at the big

151

convex windows overlooking the field and picked the mind of the young duty officer, identified by his badge as "T. Solomon."

"Are those C-One-forty-ones that are parked back there on the cargo apron?" he asked him.

"Yes, sir. Air Transport Command is gathering a squadron here, sir, for some special exercises."

Bolan asked him, "Do you have those orders?"

"No, sir. The operations officer could fill you in on that, sir. I understand there was some sort of glitch with the orders. They didn't come in until some of the aircraft had already arrived. Teletype circuits at ATC were down, or something like that."

An anomaly, perhaps.

Bolan asked, "How long have they been here?"

"They started coming in just after thirteen hundred hours, sir. I can get the log if—"

"Not necessary," Bolan grunted. "Any more large transports come in today?"

"Just the One-forty-ones, sir, but two of the super-troopers are en route from Dobbins. They just now revised their ETA to sixteen hundred hours."

Bolan checked his watch. It was now twenty minutes away from sixteen hundred hours—four o'clock by civilian count.

"I'm not familiar with your terminology, Solomon," Bolan said with a friendly smile. "What is a super-trooper?"

The guy smiled back and explained, "The C-five-A, sir, the Galaxy. Largest thing flying."

Bolan nodded and said, "Uh huh. Dobbins is the air base near Atlanta?"

"Yes, sir, at Marietta."

"Do you routinely verify these flight orders from other commands?"

"*I* don't, Colonel. I guess it's possible that someone in operations would check them."

Bolan produced a folded paper from his pocket and consulted a list of names inscribed there. "Do you know a Captain Howard Carstairs?"

"Yes, sir. Captain Carstairs will be relieving me, sir, at sixteen hundred hours."

Bolan raised his eyebrows and asked, "Duty officer?"

"Operations duty officer, yes sir."

"How well do you know Carstairs?"

"Not well, sir. He hasn't been here long."

Yeah, Bolan already knew that.

A mean-looking bird colonel came stomping in at about that point. He looked Bolan up and down and asked him, "Are you the dude with the presidential orders?"

Bolan was not pleased with this guy's attitude. He handed him the envelope without a word and turned his back on him, casting eyes but not the mind onto the field.

Behind him, a moment later, the security boss asked, "Exactly what does this mean, Colonel?"

Bolan replied, without turning around, "I presumed that you could read, Colonel. Or don't they teach you that basic skill in the Air Force?"

The guy laughed then, and it was a good sound.

Bolan turned to him with a grin, shook hands, and asked, "You ready for a bit of excitement?"

"Lord, yes," the guy said, grinning. "Did you bring me some?"

Bolan pointed to the C-141s and said, "You are to very quietly round up the flight crews from those planes and put them in chains."

The smile faded away as the security boss replied to that. "Are you serious?"

"I was born serious," Bolan told him, "and I keep finding fewer and fewer things to laugh about all the time. You also have two C-five aircraft inbound from Dobbins. I want your APs to meet those planes and take those crews in custody, also. And then there's an oncoming duty officer, a guy calling himself Carstairs. Due any minute. He's one of them, too. Arrest him. I want all those guys placed in the darkest pit you have around here and I don't want them to see daylight until I tell you different. You are to keep this entire thing under the very tightest security your command is capable of. Put your APs in ordinary uniforms and keep down the ripple effect—I want no leaks, I want utter secrecy, and I want no failure."

The guy backed onto a desk and perched his weight there, eyes hard and bright on Bolan's. After a moment, he said, "What the hell is going on?"

"You'll be given full details at the earliest possible moment. Right now I just want you to move it."

"It has something to do with the NATO event, doesn't it?"

Bolan said, "It sure has."

"Good Lord! I was just telling my boys this morning . . . this would be the perfect time for some embarrassing—damn!" He lunged across the desk and snared a telephone.

This was the man for Bolan, all right—a guy with some imagination and a willingness to act.

Another man for Bolan walked in the door at that very moment, also. Not Carstairs, though Bolan knew this was the one moment he saw him —not because of any special way the guy looked or carried himself, but solely because of the other man who accompanied him.

Bolan had his forty-five in hand and was across the room before anyone else in there could twitch —and he had the muzzle of that pistol shoved between the guy's teeth before a word could come out of there.

A man for Bolan, right—a prize man, the "captain's" chief of staff—none other than Lieutenant Thompson of Tularosa Peak and thereabouts.

Grimaldi hustled the fast-wilting Thompson away and stowed him quietly in the Cobra, there to await the pleasure of "Colonel Phoenix."

Up in the operations shack, a greatly impressed security honcho was in a huddle with that other bird colonel, firming up the Air Force interface.

Bolan gave him a card containing telephone

155

numbers and tactical radio channels as he instructed him, "You're closing your sky. Nothing flies until it has been cleared with Alice."

"That's Alice like, uh, in Wonderland?"

Bolan said, "That's the one. She's a he, though, so don't get confused about it. Not a chopper, not a trainer, not even a Piper cub hits your sky until Alice clears it. I'll give you an authentication coder to pass to your C.O. He can clear all this with Washington if it makes him feel better. Meanwhile you have a damn small sky up there, Colonel, and I'm depending on you to keep it that way."

"I should alert Air—"

Bolan growled, "Hell no, you haven't been listening to me, you alert nobody. We've been infiltrated, and nobody yet knows how high or how wide that infiltration stretches. Tell me you understand that."

"I understand that, sure," said the colonel in a hushed voice.

Bolan was making ready to break away. He paused at the door to say, "Small sky?"

"Small you haven't seen before, Army," replied the security boss. "You better hurry and get that Cobra off the ground before I seal you in."

Bolan smiled, showed the guy a clenched fist, and went away from there . . . back to the smallest sky over America.

CHAPTER TWENTY

SCENARIO DOWN

It was not what you could call an ideological war between two homelands with the stouthearts defending the faith—nor was it, either, a matter of brotherhood and loyalty to a bloodline. Harrelson's troops were simple mercenaries dedicated entirely to their own enrichment—and they were not even "bound" to the *omerta* oath of their employers.

So Mack Bolan was not at all surprised to find trooper Thompson willing to come over to the other side. Especially since Bolan had phrased the proposition in such persuasive terms.

"I don't give a damn whether you live or die, Thompson. I have no respect for your life, because you have no respect for anything whatever. I'd as soon route a bullet through your tonsils and kick your melting carcass the hell out of my ship,

157

here and now, except for one thing. I need your help.

"I think you *can* help. And I think you *will*. That's the only reason you're alive at this moment. You're the first prisoner I've taken all day—and I've taken you because I believe you are close enough to the top to have information of some value to me.

"But I don't have the time and certainly not the patience to dick around with you. I get no jollies from shredding living flesh, so I'd much rather just put it to a guy in terms of life or death.

"Now you've got this decision to make, see. It's yours entirely. Are you going to live, or are you going to die? That's the decision. But I'm not going to mislead you in this. You need to know— hell, you have a right to know, since it's your life that's at stake—you need to know that your decision is actually pitched between certain death and only a thin chance for life. But I'm offering you that chance. You decide.

"Here's the situation, flat and simple. You are sticking to me, bub, like one of my arms, until this thing is finished. If Harrelson wins, you die. Got that? He wins, you die. If I win, you live—or, at least, you don't die at my hands.

"That's simple enough, isn't it? It boils down to this: if you want to live, then you've got to stop Harrelson. Since you can't do that for yourself, your only chance is for *me* to stop Harrelson. And you better hope to God I can, if you want to live.

"I'm not going to interrogate you, guy. I'm not going to play dumb games of the flesh with you. I'm just going to take this gun out of your mouth for about thirty seconds. You start talking sense to me right away—then, okay, I leave it out and we go beat Harrelson. You don't talk quick sense, then I put the gun back in and pull the trigger.

"I can see it in your eyes. You understand. So, okay. You've got thirty seconds to decide."

It did not take the guy even ten seconds to decide, nor half that long. He'd made the decision long before that Colt forty-five came out of his tonsils.

It did, though, require a couple of seconds to get the saliva under control and to make his speech intelligible. Beyond that, there was not the slightest hesitancy in his response.

"What time is it now?"

"It's ten past four. You have a date with somebody?"

"There will be a diversion shot at five o'clock. You'll need to stop that, first."

"What kind of shot?"

"Nerve gas. Just enough to create a range emergency. Meteorologist says it should drift northeasterly across the flats at about ten miles per hour with a kill zone of maybe three hundred yards across."

"How does this happen?"

"We quietly took control of Complex Three at nine o'clock this morning. The gas was canistered in the inert mode, for display only, so the brass could see what it looked like. We added the cata-lyst and loaded it aboard a Lance SRBM, one of the latest configurations. The Lance is scheduled for a demo shot Friday morning. It will be acci-dentally launched at five o'clock today."

"About a seventy mile on that baby," Grimaldi said worriedly.

"The target is not that far," Thompson quickly informed them. "The bird will go in a bit north of Tularosa, about twenty miles inside the range. We calculated a possible risk factor of less than one percent for contamination reaching the civil-ian sector."

"How would you like that factor," Grimaldi inquired angrily, "if your wife and kids lived in Tularosa?"

"The forecast winds—"

The pilot snorted that response away. *"Fore-cast . . ."*

Bolan said, "Okay so we have a diversion scheduled for five o'clock. Then what?"

But Thompson had not left the "diversion" be-hind, yet. "That gas should get bottled into the mountains," he said, speaking really to Grimaldi and maybe trying to establish the idea that he was not that much a monster. "It can be neutralized long before there's any danger to the populace. We merely wanted the range emergency confusion factor."

"Then what?" Bolan persisted.

"We've been working a shell game for about a week. Ninety percent of the weapons slated for the

NATO event have been completely disassembled and crated for trans-shipment."

"To where?"

"We start ferrying it over to Holloman at five o'clock, under cover of the range emergency. There are a number of large air transports, fully crewed with our own people, waiting and ready for a legitimate training flight to Puerto Rico. We will refuel there and go on across the Atlantic to an as-yet-undisclosed destination somewhere in North Africa. I don't know the plan from that point."

The guy was beginning to sound like a press release. Bolan inquired, "Who does know?"

Thompson shrugged and showed the palms of his hands. "I suppose the captain knows. Or the banker. I just know that the training mission is supposed to terminate at Puerto Rico. We kluged it for an extension to an air base in Spain. But it will divert at the last minute to somewhere in North Africa."

"By what method do you ferry the stuff to Holloman?"

"We have four Chinooks loaded with the hot stuff—you know, warheads. The nuts and bolts systems will go by truck convoy. They will move out through Rancho Jacundo and down Highway Fifty-four through Alamogordo en route to Holloman."

Grimaldi said, "These guys don't miss a trick, do they? Ask him about Camp Strong."

Thompson did not need an interpreter. He told

Grimaldi, "We accelerated beyond Camp Strong." His eyes flashed to Bolan. "A tribute to your influence, sir. The captain chose not to risk—well, we went to the acceleration contingency. The original plan was to accidentally shoot down the observation planes, which would be carrying the NATO visitors, as they toured the range prior to the demonstrations. That was on tap for tomorrow."

The pilot commented, sourly, "No worry about risk factors for that one, eh?"

Thompson smiled solemnly and replied, "If you mean would the captain weep over a general's spilled blood, no, there was no worry. He's still quite bitter about Vietnam. So are many of us. Aren't you? They sent us into a war they never intended to win. It wasn't really a war, was it? It was a political caucus."

Bolan sighed and punched in the Tac channel. "Alice," he called.

"Go."

"Have you been contacted by Holloman?"

"Yeah. Just finished an interesting conversation with the commanding general. Why didn't I think of that?"

"Here's something better to think about. A range emergency is scheduled for five o'clock. That's today—in, uh, forty-five minutes from now. You'd better get a hot-hot team over to Complex Three. A Lance missile has been salted for CBW. It will be accidentally launched at five. Unless someone gets there first."

"Someone will," Brognola promised, and he quit that connection immediately.

"At six o'clock," Thompson went on, unprodded, "the air transports should be on their way. Once they are airborne, the national communications link at El Paso will blink out." He smiled, but without much humor. "Another confusion event. All the national telecommunications between east and west will be disrupted. So a few million homes will miss part of the evening news. And telephone calls. But just briefly. When they make the switchover to ComSat, everyone will settle back happily. But another hand will be rattling the microwaves."

Bolan nodded his head and commented, "That's why the anxiety over the California link."

"Some of it, yes. A confusion event of your own, Colonel. We bridged that without too much inconvenience, however. There are other points between here and California to fill the gap."

Bolan said, "You'll be telling someone else about that, all of that, later. Right now I want to know what your contingency is for a sealed sky over Holloman."

"For what?"

"Your flight crews are in chains and your planes are grounded. There you sit with tons of stolen weapons. What do you do now?"

Thompson replied, "I don't believe that eventuality is covered, sir."

"Then," Bolan told him, "you've got a hell of a glitch in your scenario."

"Sir?"

"This is no drill, soldier. You *do* have a sealed sky over Holloman."

The guy smiled with genuine good nature this time. "Then I'd have to say you've won the game, Colonel Phoenix. Or is it Colonel Bolan?"

That title, used with that name, sounded strange indeed to the ex-career sergeant from 'Nam—even from those lips and in this context.

"It's *Sergeant* Bolan, Lieutenant," he told the guy. .

"Well, I used to be *Major* Thompson, sir," the guy told him with a sober smile. "And I'd feel privileged to serve under you anytime, anywhere . . . Colonel."

Flattery was not going to get the guy anywhere . . . but Bolan did feel a pain for military excellence gone awry.

And he had not won the game, yet.

Not all of it.

Still lying ahead was the final showdown with another fine military mind gone crazy.

"How many people does Harrelson have?" he asked Thompson.

"On the scene . . . not counting air crews . . . about two hundred strong."

"How many of those are combat people?"

"Less than fifty, scattered all over the range."

"They'll be closing, though, at five o'clock."

"They should be closing right now, yes. I see what you mean. I'd call it fifty good combat troops."

"He had a hell of a lot more than that in Colorado."

"Yes, sir. But he lost a hell of a lot more than that in Colorado, too. They're not easy to replace. And about half of the survivors drifted away soon after, I understand."

Bolan wondered aloud, "Were you with him in Colorado?"

"No, sir. I came in with the new wave."

"Did you have a brother, then, in Colorado?"

"You must be thinking of a man named Thomas. He was staff, too, but not the same name. He died."

Bolan muttered, "Yes, I know." A moment later: "Why, Thompson?"

"Why what?"

"What the *hell* are you doing here?"

The guy shifted his gaze, intertwined his fingers, and replied, "It seems that nobody else wanted me, sir."

A good answer.

No . . . a bad answer. What nobody else wanted was what the guy did best.

And that was a tragic answer.

They were bivouacked in a dry gulch along the north base of Tularosa Peak—and God it was an impressive collection.

Four huge Chinook cargo 'copters, all buttoned up and awaiting the lift-off command, were at the head of the parade. Behind them were lined two jeeps, three personnel carriers, and a long convoy of military ground transports, followed to the rear by two more jeeps.

Each of those jeeps boasted a machine gun mount on the rear deck—and they were manned.

Hovering above it all was a Bell Huey Cobra identical to Bolan's gunship. The original plan had evidently called for three of those gunships to ride the airspace above the convoy.

They had been prepared to punch through whatever disorganized opposition might be encountered along that route. Even now, two Hueys shy, it was a formidable force.

The ground transports were of the type designed to be driven right aboard a waiting air transport. So it could have been a slick operation, sure. The Chinooks would have gone ahead on their own, no doubt, and their hot cargo would have been transferred to the waiting planes by the time the ground convoy hit the scene. They could be buttoned up and gone within a matter of minutes after the convoy arrived at Holloman.

It could have worked beautifully, sure.

But Bolan had other plans for that bunch.

It was precisely seventeen hundred hours when Grimaldi slid the Cobra into the airspace above the bivouac area. He had a hot position on the other gunship and Bolan knew that he would keep it that way. With all the other commotion around there, it seemed likely only Harrelson's ship was immediately aware that someone new had come to play.

Bolan punched into their tac net to announce, "You lose again, Captain."

That Arkansas drawl came back at him calm and unruffled: "You can't lose the game on the opening kick-off, Hawg."

"Better think of it as a two-minute drill," Bolan advised him. "The ball is on your one-foot line and you've used all your time-outs."

That other Huey was trying to get position on Grimaldi, with no immediate success.

Meanwhile Harrelson was telling his old hell-grounds companion, "But you haven't seen my gimmick plays yet, Hawg. There's still time for you to concede the game and come on over to my yard for champagne and Texas steaks."

Grimaldi warned, "It's getting tight."

Bolan radioed that other ship, "You offered me better than that the last time out, Captain. Is the market dropping?"

"Hell no, the market is not dropping. Tell you what, name your own reward. How 'bout that?"

It had come down to now or maybe never for Grimaldi. His tight voice hit that channel with a snap. "Hold it right there, dude! Another foot of altitude and I send you a hot golden goose!"

The other craft abruptly stabilized.

Bolan radioed, "You have the shoe on the wrong foot, Cap. This parley is for your sake, not mine. If you're wondering why it's past seventeen hundred and you're hearing no range emergency signals, I can rest your mind on that number. There will be no CBW on the range today. You should also be made aware that the skies over Holloman are closed. Your bogus flight crews are in chains and your air transports are now manned by the Air Police. You have a single option. Put that bird down and step outside where I can see you. Kill all engines and move your personnel out of that gulch and into open country. There's a force out there waiting to greet them. Not with champagne and steaks, but I can promise your boys bread and water, at least, for a while. You put it down right now or my friend the heat jockey will put you down, his way. Right now, Harrelson!"

Others had been listening in on that death moment parley. Another carrier came in and a shaken voice pleaded, "Do it, Cappy. There'll always be a next time."

Another chimed in with a vote. "They got us cold, Cap. Let's quit."

Brognola's marshals chose that moment to expose themselves at the rim of the dry gulch. They wore flak jackets and toted big submachine guns. There must have been a hundred of them lining that rim.

And Frank Harrelson chose that moment for his decision. His gunship lurched skyward and dropped her tail, seeking a hot line to Bolan's ship. A missile zipped away from there, inscribing a fiery path across Grimaldi's bow and another quickly followed, to also miss by inches.

Grimaldi was reacting to the maneuver, however, jockeying quickly and sending a pair of answering firebirds whizzing down in instant response. The firing angle had been momentarily lost, though, and both birds zipped past the bucking Huey to plow into a ground transport directly below it.

Bolan yelled into the intercom, "Fifty!" and sent a wreath of fire encircling the other Cobra's tail section.

Harrelson's tail rotor flew away on its own independent program and the big gunship immediately lost stability, going into a slide to starboard and beginning to slowly windmill around the main rotor.

Down below, troopers were spilling from that line of vehicles and stretching both hands toward the small sky above their heads. The Chinooks were also shutting down, and people were moving quickly away from the big ships.

Harrelson's Huey slid around the face of Tularosa Peak in a windmilling climb to nowhere.

Grimaldi's face was tight and sad as he commented to his partner, "No place to go from there, man. No place at all."

"Stay on them," Bolan instructed.

They followed the disabled craft in a crazy plunge eastward along an aerial path, which seemed to be headed straight toward Rancho Jacundo.

That's where it was headed, all right, and that was where it came down—a scant fifty yards from the adobe huts. It hit with a hell of a bang and sent crumpled parts of itself scattering across the rocky ground, spilling bodies and other debris across bandit country.

Grimaldi set down at a safe distance and a grim-eyed Mack Bolan strode across the impact area for a close inspection of the crash site.

None of those bodies had belonged to Frank Harrelson—not the spilled ones.

The ruptured fuselage was draped across a large rock and the odor of released fuel was strong in the air. He found Harrelson there, seated upright in the wreckage, strapped to a seat that was no longer connected to anything else.

The eyes were open and they were watching the careful approach of Mack Bolan.

That bloodied mouth opened also, forming words that would have sounded straight from Arkansas if there'd been any sound at all.

He was twenty feet out when a sheet of flame erupted across the line of vision, concealing everything within that wreckage from outside view, then quickly scattering the whole mess in a puffing explosion that sent Bolan to the ground, covering up against flaming debris.

He returned to the gunship and climbed aboard.

Grimaldi tightly commented, "That was tough."

And Lt. Thompson found his first words of the strike. "Hell of a way to go, isn't it? But I guess there's no doubt now, Colonel, that you won this one."

Bolan settled into his seat and fastened the harness. He lit a cigarette and watched his hands shake for a moment. He looked at Thompson, then dropped the gaze as he responded to that comment. "Nobody, Major," he said quietly, "won this one."

Well, it would have been a hell of a scenario in the flesh, for damn sure.

Nerve gas drifting across New Mexico toward Tucumcari and maybe getting there via an Indian reservation—a final word to the Apaches, eh?

Then panic throughout the southwest: communications piracy briefly splitting the country apart; manipulation of emergency communications networks; an anxious NATO alliance wondering where all the generals had gone; perhaps even a brief national emergency in the confusion of the moment, with strategic missiles and nuclear bombers and subs poising for a response to something dreaded but not really happening.

For the final stroke, no one anywhere actually aware of the real peril for perhaps days, or until those forbidden weapons created a bona fide emergency for another nation or two . . . then, maybe, for the whole trembling world.

Yeah, Phil, it was a hell of a scenario.

And Mack Bolan was not a damned bit sorry that the crazy bastard had not lived to see its flesh.

In the very deepest regions of this man, though, there was a genuine and terrible sorrow that Frank Harrelson had not survived its single flaw.

EPILOGUE

"We have Minotti on ice," Brognola reported. "But we found him with clean hands and I really doubt that we can make anything stick. I believe the best way to handle that guy would be just to turn him loose and let his own people have their will with him. It would probably be much harsher treatment than anything he'd find with us. I take it this whole thing with Harrelson was his baby—I mean from Colorado on. I've had some people back east checking this thing out all day and it seems there was a connection between those two predating Colorado by several months."

Bolan smiled sourly and commented, "Then he stuck the family treasury for gobs of bucks poorly spent. Maybe you're right. Go ahead. Send him home in tatters. For sure, that won't be doing the guy any favors."

Brognola seemed a bit startled by the easy argument. "Okay. We'll do that, then. Uh, listen—I've had people in Dallas all day, too. We, uh, went ahead and swept the place clean."

Bolan quietly said, "Okay."

That, too, apparently came to Brognola as a surprising response. He fidgeted for a moment, then said, "So there's no damage to your time-table. We can go on with—"

"Wait, Hal," Bolan said, holding up a hand in quiet protest. "I believe I want to rethink my position."

"Well, now wait a minute. I thought we had all this ironed out. You're going to put me in a hell of an uncomfortable posture if I have to go back to the White House and tell that man . . . well, dammit, I'd almost rather change places with Marco."

Bolan sighed tiredly and said, "I'm not welshing on the deal, Hal. I just want to make sure I know where I am and where it's heading. I need to breathe on my own for a while, think my own thoughts, make my own decisions."

"That's fair enough," the fed said, though obviously not entirely satisfied with the response. "How much time do you need for this?"

"I'll meet you in Florida tomorrow, as planned."

"Oh! Okay, swell. Hell, I thought you were—okay, tomorrow as planned."

Bolan focused his tired gaze on April Rose. "Understand?" he quietly inquired.

She nodded the lovely head and replied, "Sure. It's okay. See you tomorrow."

He got up and went out of there.

Grimaldi was waiting for him in the plane. Bolan stepped aboard and said, "We go."

"Fine. But where the hell?"

"Just pick a spot, Jack. Anywhere between here and Pensacola where it's quiet and peaceful."

"You're mad, huh?"

"Mad as hell," Bolan replied in a soft voice.

"Thought so. You've been mad all day. Not like you, pal. Who you mad at? Why?"

Bolan did not know why, nor did he know with any certainty at whom the anger was directed. At himself, perhaps. Or maybe at Frank Harrelson . . . or Bob Thompson . . . Phil Jordan, Mary Valdez, the whole crazy pattern . . . or maybe none of it.

He just knew that he was mad as hell, deep down where it really felt.

And this was only Wednesday.

Dear Reader:

The Pinnacle Books editors strive to select and produce books that are exciting, entertaining and readable . . . no matter what the category. From time to time we will attempt to discover what you, the reader, think about a particular book or series.

Now that you've finished reading this volume in *The Executioner* series, we'd like to find out what you liked, or didn't like, about this story. We'll share your opinions with the author and discuss them as we plan future books. This will result in books that you will find more to your liking. As in fine art and good cooking a matter of taste is involved; and for you, of course, it is *your* taste that is most important to you. For Don Pendleton, and the Pinnacle editors, it is not the critics' reviews and publicity that have been most rewarding, it is the un-ending stream of readers' mail. Here is where we discover what readers like, what they *feel* about a story, and what they find memorable. So, do help us in becoming a little more knowledgeable in providing you with the kind of stories you like. Here's how . . .

WIN BOOKS . . . AND $200! Please fill out the following pages and mail them as indicated. Every week, for twelve weeks following publication, the editors will choose, at random, a reader's name from all the questionnaires received. The twelve lucky readers will receive $25 worth of paperbacks *and* become an official entry in our 1979 Pinnacle Books Reader Sweepstakes. The winner of this sweepstakes drawing will receive a Grand Prize of $200, the inclusion of their name in a forthcoming Pinnacle Book (as a special acknowledgment, possibly even as a character!), and several other local prizes to be announced to each initial winner. As a further inducement to send in your questionnaire *now,* we will also send the first 25 replies received a free book by return mail! Here's a chance to talk to the author and editors, voice your opinions, and win some great prizes, too!

READER SURVEY

NOTE: Please feel free to expand on any of these questions on a separate page, or to express yourself on any aspect of your thoughts on reading . . . but do be sure to include this entire questionnaire with any such letters.

1. Are you glad you bought this book, and did it live up to your expectations?

2. What was it about this book that induced you to buy it?
    (A. The title_____) (B. The author's name_____)
    (C. A friend's recommendation_____)
    (D. The cover art_____)
    (E. The cover description_____)
    (F. Subject matter_____) (G. Advertisement_____)
    (H. Heard author on TV or radio_____)
    (I. Read a previous book in this series_____ . . .
        which ones? _____)
    (J. Bookstore display_____)
    (K. Other? _____

3. What is the book you read just before this one?

    And how would you rate it with this volume in *The Executioner* series? _____

4. What is the very next book you plan to read?

    How did you decide on that? _____

5. Where did you buy this volume in *The Executioner* series? _____

(Name and address of store, please):

_____

_____

6. Where do you buy the majority of your paperbacks? _____

7. What seems to be the major factor that persuades you to buy a certain book?

_____

8. How many books do you buy each month?

_____

9. Do you ever write letters to the author or publisher . . . and why? _____

_____

10. About how many hours a week do you spend reading books? _____ How many hours a week watching television? _____

11. What other spare-time activity do you enjoy most? _____ For how many hours a week? _____

12. Which magazines do you read regularly? . . . in order of your preference _____,

_____, _____,

_____

13. Of your favorite magazine, what is it that you like best about it? _____

_____

14. What is your favorite television show of the past year or so? _____

15. What is your favorite motion picture of the past year or so? _____

16. What is the most disappointing television show you've seen lately? _____

17. What is the most disappointing motion picture you've seen lately? _____

18. What is the most disappointing book you've read lately? _____

19. Are there authors that you like so well that you read *all* their books? _____
    Who are they? _____

20. And can you explain *why* you like their books so much? _____
    _____
    _____

21. Which particular books by these authors do you like best? _____
    _____

22. Did you read Taylor Caldwell's *Captains and Kings*?_____ Did you watch it on television?_____
    Which did you do first? _____

23. Did you read John Jakes' *The Bastard*? _____
    Did you watch it on TV?_____ Which first?_____
    Have you read any of the other books in John Jakes' Bicentennial Series? _____
    What do you think of them? _____

24. Did you read James Michener's *Centennial?*
    _____ Did you watch it on TV? _____ Which first?
    _____

25. Did you read Irwin Shaw's *Rich Man, Poor Man*? _____ Did you watch it on TV? _____
    Which first? _____

26. Of all the recent books you've read, or films you've seen, are there any that you would compare in any way to *The Executioner*? _____

27. With series books that you like, how often would you like to read them . . . (a) twice a year _____? (b) three times a year _____? (c) every other month _____? (d) every month _____? (e) other _____?

28. What is your favorite book character or series of all time? _____
And why? _____

29. Do you collect any paperback series? _____
Which ones? _____

30. What do you like *best* about *The Executioner* series? _____

31. And what don't you like about it . . . if anything? _____

32. Have you read any books in *The Destroyer* series? _____ And what is your opinion of them?
_____

33. Have you read any books in the Nick Carter *Killmaster* series? _____ Opinion? _____
_____

34. Have you read any books in *The Death Merchant* series? _____ Opinion? _____
_____

35. Have you read any books in *The Penetrator* series? _____ Opinion? _____

36. Have you read any books in *The Edge* series? _____ Opinion? _____
_____

37. Have you read any books in *The Butcher* series? _____ Opinion? _____
_____

38. Have you read any books in the *Louis L'Amour* western series? _____ Opinion? _____
_____

39. Have you read any books in the *Travis McGee* series? Opinion? _____
_____

40. Have you read any books in the *Matt Helm* series? _____ Opinion? _____
_____

41. Have you read any books in the *Carter Brown* mystery series? _____ Opinion? _____
_____

42. Rank the following descriptions of *The Executioner* series as you feel they are best defined:

	Excellent	*Okay*	*Poor*
A. A sense of reality	_____	_____	_____
B. Suspense	_____	_____	_____
C. Intrigue	_____	_____	_____
D. Sexuality	_____	_____	_____
E. Violence	_____	_____	_____
F. Romance	_____	_____	_____
G. History	_____	_____	_____
H. Characterization	_____	_____	_____
I. Scenes, events	_____	_____	_____
J. Pace, readability	_____	_____	_____
K. Dialogue	_____	_____	_____
L. Style	_____	_____	_____

43. What do you do with your paperbacks after you've read them? _____

_____

44. Do you buy paperbacks in any of the following categories, and approximately how many do you buy in a year?

   A. Contemporary fiction _____
   B. Historical romance _____
   C. Family saga _____
   D. Romance (like Harlequin) _____
   E. Romantic suspense _____
   F. Gothic romance _____
   G. Occult novels _____
   H. War novels _____
   I. Action/adventure novels (like *this* book) _____
   J. "Bestsellers" _____
   K. Science fiction _____
   L. Mystery _____
   M. Westerns _____
   N. Nonfiction _____
   O. Biography _____
   P. How-To books _____
   O. Other _____

45. And, lastly, some profile data on *you* the reader . . .

   A. Age: 12–16_____ 17–20_____ 21–30_____
   31–40_____ 41–50_____ 51–60_____
   61 or over_____

   B. Occupation: _____

C. Education level; check last grade completed:
10 _____ 11 _____ 12 _____ Freshman _____
Sophomore _____ Junior _____ Senior _____
Graduate School _____, plus any specialized
schooling _____

D. Your average annual gross income: Under
$10,000 _____ $10,000–$15,000 _____
$15,000–$20,000 _____ $20,000–
$30,000 _____ $30,000–$50,000 _____
Above $50,000 _____

E. Did you read a lot as a child? _____ Do you
recall your favorite childhood novel? _____
_____

F. Do you find yourself reading more or less
than you did five years ago? _____

G. Do you read hardcover books? _____ How
often? _____ If so, are they books that you
buy? _____ borrow? _____ or trade? _____ Or
other? _____

H. Does the imprint (Pinnacle, Avon, Bantam,
etc.) make any difference to you when con-
sidering a paperback purchase? _____

I. Have you ever bought paperbacks by mail
directly from the publisher? _____ And do you
like to buy books that way? _____

J. Would you be interested in buying paperbacks via a book club or subscription program? _____ And, in your opinion, what would

be the best reasons for doing so? _____
_____ . . . the problems in
doing so? _____

K. Is there something that you'd like to see
writers or publishers do for you as a reader
of paperbacks? _____
_____

L. Would you be interested in joining an *Executioner* fan club? _____
_____

M. If so, which of the following items would interest you most:

	GREAT IDEA!	DEPENDS . . .	FORGET IT!
Monthly Newsletter	_____	_____	_____
Membership card	_____	_____	_____
Membership scroll (for framing)	_____	_____	_____
T-shirt	_____	_____	_____
Sweat shirt	_____	_____	_____
Windbreaker jacket	_____	_____	_____
Poster	_____	_____	_____
Decal	_____	_____	_____
Other ideas?	_____		

(On those items above that you *do* like, indicate what you think a fair price would be.)

THANK YOU FOR TAKING THE TIME TO REPLY TO THIS, THE FIRST PUBLIC READER SURVEY IN PAPERBACK HISTORY!

NAME _____ PHONE _____

ADDRESS _____

CITY _____ STATE _____ ZIP _____

Please return this questionnaire to:

The Editors; Survey Dept. ES
Pinnacle Books, Inc.
2029 Century Park East
Los Angeles, CA 90067

the EXECUTIONER
by Don Pendleton

Over 20 million copies sold!

Mack Bolan considers the entire world a Mafia jungle and himself the final judge, jury, and executioner. He tough, deadly, and the most wanted man in America. When he's at war, nothing and nobody can stop him.